CLIFFTOPPERS
THE ARROWHEAD MOOR
ADVENTURE

Look out for more

CLIFFTOPPERS

The Stormy Point Adventure

The Thorn Island Adventure

CLIFFTOPPERS
THE ARROWHEAD MOOR
ADVENTURE

FLEUR HITCHCOCK

nosy
crow

First published in the UK in 2019 by Nosy Crow Ltd
The Crow's Nest, 14 Baden Place
Crosby Row, London SE1 1YW, UK

Nosy Crow and associated logos are trademarks and/or registered
trademarks of Nosy Crow Ltd

A CIP catalogue record for this book is available from the British Library.

Printed and bound in Great Britain by Clays Ltd, Elcograf S.p.A.
Typeset by Tiger Media

Papers used by Nosy Crow are made from wood grown in
sustainable forests.

ISBN: 978 1 78800 469 5

www.nosycrow.com

For Lazlo and Ida

CHAPTER 1

Ava unlocked the bike shed and hauled the bikes out into the soggy yard. It had rained all night, but now birds bounced through the puddles and chattered, and it felt as if, with the coming of the Easter holidays, spring could burst out at any second.

"Mine!" shouted her brother, Josh, grabbing the smallest bike before it fell.

"Mine," echoed their cousin Chloe, catching the one with the painted flowers on it.

"And mine!" said Ava, leaping on to the biggest

bike and pedalling like mad so that it wouldn't fall over.

"Bella! Here!" shouted Josh as a white dog shot out of the shed in pursuit of a terrified rat. "Let's go! I'm hungry."

"Hang on, you lot, let me just check something," Aiden, the second oldest of the four cousins, called from behind a large map of the Dragon Peninsula.

"Oh my god, Aiden," said Ava. "We want to go have this picnic, like, today!"

"I'm only…" Aiden pushed his glasses up his nose and unfolded another piece of the map.

Chloe sighed.

Josh sighed theatrically.

Aiden ignored them, folded the map back into his backpack, picked up a black bike from the ground and brushed the cobwebs off it. He did an experimental circuit of the yard and pointed up the hill.

"Wait!" Grandma burst into the yard from the kitchen. "You've forgotten your lunch. Grandpa's made cheese sandwiches for you, Chloe, and it's tuna mayonnaise for the rest of you. Some fried chicken, Josh – and here's emergency funds," she said, handing a picnic bag to Aiden and money to Ava. "Don't let Bella eat any chocolate, and we've got the Drake's Bay Film Association here today, lots of very boring people, so no need to come back until the sun's going to bed."

"Thanks, Grandma," shouted Chloe. "See you later."

Grandma waved them off as Bella raced round the side of the farmhouse and joined Josh at the front.

As they climbed the hill away from the farm, the clouds parted and strong shafts of yellow sunlight broke through, shining down on to the lighthouse and the patchwork quilt of fields that surrounded Drake's Bay and transforming the landscape. The tarmac dried instantly.

A second later, steam rose from the freshly washed fields, and Ava felt wonderfully free as she did every time they were allowed to come and stay here. She breathed in the fresh air and sensed the excitement start to build. It was always good at the farm. Somehow things always happened when all four cousins were together.

She stopped to strip off her waterproof and

watched as the sunbeams turned the water in Drake's Bay from grey to shimmering silver. She smiled. All this was a million miles away from her and Josh's life in Birmingham, and she suspected from Aiden's in London. And although Chloe had a garden, she didn't have any brothers or sisters, or anyone to hang out with. All of them had busy parents, but their grandparents seemed to have all the time in the world.

It was heaven.

"Come on, sis. You're taking ages!" Josh yelled over his shoulder.

Ava stood on her pedals and pushed the bike up the hill. Ahead of her the hedges became lower and the landscape flattened, and soon Ava was racing along, feeling the sun's heat on her arms and legs and the spring breeze cooling her face.

"Left," shouted Aiden.

They swung left, cycling almost in a line with Josh leading the way, and soon reached a T-junction with a big brown sign pointing right to *Arrowhead Moor House and Gardens*.

"Right!" yelled Josh, pedalling off towards the house.

Bella followed, strolling into the middle of the road and stopping to sniff the tarmac.

Just then a red open-top sports car shot over the brow of the hill.

"Bella!" screamed Aiden.

BEEP. Screeeeeeeeeeeeeeeeeech!

The car skidded to a halt, missing Bella by a dog's length, and stopped just in front of Chloe's front wheel.

"Hey!" shouted Josh. "You nearly—"

"Idiots!" shouted the woman behind the wheel. "Get that stupid dog off the road!"

"Sorry, we'll keep her on the lead," said Aiden, his freckled face turning bright red. "But … perhaps … perhaps you were driving too fast, and perhaps…" He pointed to the mobile phone in her hand.

"Oh, for goodness' sake!" Without another word the woman threw the phone on the passenger seat, wrenched the wheel round and whizzed off towards Arrowhead Moor House.

Dropping her bike, Chloe ran over to Bella and gave her a hug. "You naughty dog, you're supposed to look when you cross the road. We nearly lost you."

Bella responded by barking at the car as it disappeared over the horizon.

"What a…" started Chloe, unable to find the words to finish her sentence.

"Exactly," said Ava.

Josh took a little red notebook from his pocket and wrote down the number plate of the car. *Going too fast. Using mobile phone while driving.* "Can we do the picnic now?" he said. "I'm starving."

CHAPTER 2

Aiden was happy to amble along at the back, half his mind thinking about the car that had just missed Bella – and actually Chloe – and wondering why anyone would want to drive so fast on the moor. There was nothing up here apart from nature and sunshine. It was far too beautiful to race around in a car. He stopped and stretched his arms wide, letting the others get well ahead of him before reaching for the handlebars and pedalling crazily to catch up.

The landscape changed from moorland to

fields and then back to moorland. Hedges appeared and disappeared as they cycled higher. The sun hid behind a cloud and a steady mizzle started up again, just enough to be refreshing but not to soak him. His glasses misted over and he paused to wipe them clean. Above, he heard a bird singing, and he wondered if it was a lark. He had a feeling that they lived on moors. He was still thinking about larks when they cycled through a small wood and passed the Three Witches pub on their left.

It was a dark pub with tiny diamond-pane windows. A few run-down sheds collected around its untidy yard. It wasn't welcoming at the best of times, and right now in the rain it actually looked sinister. A hand-painted sign advertising rooms hung over the door, but Aiden couldn't imagine any tourists staying there on purpose. The beds would be lumpy and there would be cobwebs.

The others raced on ahead, but Aiden slowed. He needed to clean his glasses properly, so he was almost at a halt when he spotted the red open-top car parked alongside the pub. Resting his bike against a collapsing shed, he took off his glasses and wiped them carefully on his T-shirt. It gave him an excellent opportunity to take a really good look at the car.

He was thinking of wandering over to peer in when the door to the pub slammed open.

"So I expect absolute silence on your part," said a woman to someone he couldn't see.

It was her – the woman who'd nearly squished Bella. Now he could see her properly she looked very out of place, like someone who had just stepped out of a department store in New York. She wore red high heels and a shiny black mac pulled tight at the waist. Her hair was very black, dyed black, and she was now wearing dark glasses. Why would you wear dark glasses when it was raining?

"I'll be back later. Take any messages," she ordered.

He crouched by his bike and pretended to check the tyres, listening all the while. A second later, she revved the engine and the car shot past him into the lane. Tyres skidding, it headed towards Arrowhead Moor House.

He watched the spray behind the car disappear as it went down a dip in the road. The woman was driving far too fast. No wonder she'd nearly hit them.

Thinking about strange behaviour and sports cars and women looking out of place in red high heels, Aiden climbed back on his bike and headed down the road, pushing his legs a little harder to catch up with the others. He knew he was approaching the house when the first cherry trees smothered in blossom began to line the road. Then there were neat barns and fields of tiny lambs, and finally huge terracotta pots jammed full of bold orange tulips. By the time he reached the others they were already in the queue for tickets.

"So, four of you? Who's the oldest? Who's got the money?" said the man behind the counter.

"She has," said Josh, pointing at Ava. "She's twelve, he's eleven, and she –" he pointed at Chloe – "she's only a bit older than me."

"I'm nine," said Chloe. "He's eight."

"Nearly nine," said Josh.

"Ah. Out for a picnic, are you?" The man nodded at the bag Aiden was carrying.

"Yes, and we're starving. Where can we eat our

picnic?" asked Josh.

The man looked over his glasses at Josh and smiled. "The picnic area is just round the back of the house, on the cobbles. And when you're done, see if you can find the missing sheep. They were taken from here in the night."

Josh pinched his brows together and took the entrance tickets that the man held out. "Sheep?" he said.

"Yup, from our farm buildings. Someone stole twenty pedigree ewes. All of them are about to lamb. There's been quite a hoo-ha about them."

Josh wrote this in his notebook.

"Are they worth a lot?" asked Chloe.

"Several thousand pounds apparently…" The man peered past Chloe at something on the far side of the room. "Is that your dog?"

In the minute they'd been standing there, Bella had found a packet of biscuits behind one of the counters and was already crunching through the packaging.

Josh opened his mouth to ask something else, but Ava took him by the elbow and Aiden grabbed Bella by the collar and they dragged them both out of the visitor centre.

"Here," Ava said, handing Josh the picnic blanket. "Go and find us somewhere to eat."

CHAPTER 3

Full of Grandpa Edward's almost-as-good-as-Grandpa-Winston's jerk chicken, Josh left the others examining the rest of the picnic and headed off to explore and see if he could find anything out about the missing sheep. He was surprised that a bunch of pooey sheep were worth thousands, but that made the hunt more worthwhile. The sun shone, the air was fresh and Josh felt good. Skipping over the grass, he leaped a molehill and started jumping between the tussocks. Then he noticed that a herd of curious cows were following him.

"Ooh!" he said, swerving to avoid them and racing towards the long iron fence that separated the deer park from the gardens. The cows sped up, tails swinging, breathing heavily through wet nostrils as they followed him over the lumpy grass.

Josh changed gear. He moved from lollop to sprint, bouncing across the turf, forcing his legs to go faster and faster.

The cows became more interested, and the first excited cow broke into a trot.

"Yow," said Josh, leaping for the fence.

He made it over just as the whole herd shuffled into a stampede.

"Ha!" he shouted when he was safe on the other side.

He headed for the stream that he knew ran down from the house across the moor. Dodging round the walls of the garden, Josh ducked under a strand of wire and, balancing on tussocks, made his way towards the stile and the small coppice of trees that he knew surrounded the stream. It was a natural enclosure. It would be a fine place to hide sheep.

Cows' hooves had made deep dark brown sucky holes in the turf, which joined together to make ponds and even lakes. He teetered on the edge of a particularly large pooey sea before launching himself across the few grassy islands that lay between him and the stile.

"Ah!" He grabbed at the wooden crossbeam and only lost the front of one trainer to the brown goo. "Yay!" he shouted as he got both feet on to the plank of the stile. He jumped over the fence, straight into a stream hidden under the long grass.

"Aaargh!" The water was freezing and Josh leaped out the other side, jumping over trailing ivy and scrambling up stones until he reached the edge of the clump of trees. He stopped to examine his feet. Sopping wet trainers with sopping wet socks. He sat on the ground to empty the water from his shoes and looked up to see a woman standing in another group of trees, slightly further away from the house, looking around her.

Josh paused, a shoe in his hand. She was definitely checking to see if anyone was watching.

Still holding his shoe, he backed into the trees, nestling under an overhanging branch and pulling his sweatshirt hood over his head. If he stayed really still, she probably wouldn't see him.

She was tall, wearing a black mac and stupid red shiny shoes. Nearly everyone else here was wearing walking boots and green-coloured waterproofs, so she looked really out of place.

From under his hood Josh watched as she hooked a black holdall over a branch as if to keep it safe while she leaned over to inspect the mud on her shoes. The branch bowed under the weight. She remained looking at her shoe for the longest time, inspecting her other shoe too, and then stepped away, leaving the bag.

Instinctively Josh sprang up and raced over the lumpy grass. "Hey! Miss!" he shouted. "You've forgotten your bag!"

The woman swung her gaze towards him and for a second she looked as if she was going to run. Her expression went from bewildered to furious to fake happy.

Josh narrowed his eyes. *The woman from the speeding car.*

"On the tree, there…" Josh pointed at the little group of trees and the black zipped bag dangling from the branch.

"Oh! Goodness me," said the woman, her funny,

trilling laugh dancing over the meadow. "How silly of me and how helpful of you."

She took a couple of paces back and yanked the bag from the branch before striding, as much as she could stride in her silly shoes, back towards Arrowhead Moor House.

CHAPTER 4

"Eeew," said Chloe, picking at a huge lump of chocolate icing that had dripped from her slice of cake on to her jeans. "I'm going to have to go and wash this off."

A moment later, Josh came squelching back towards them, waving his arms.

"Oh my god, Josh. You've been so long that Chloe's wandered off. What happened?" said his sister crossly.

Out of breath, Josh threw himself on to the bench. "Got to tell you ... that woman," he puffed.

"Behaving like…" He pulled the corners of his mouth down and widened his eyes.

"Is that s'posed to be scary?" asked Ava.

"Weird. Hey!" He pointed at Grandpa's chocolate cake. "Can I have a bit of that?" Aiden handed him a chunk. "She hung a really huge heavy bag in a tree in the middle of nowhere. Maybe she's the sheep thief."

"What woman?" asked Ava, moving the cake out of Bella and Josh's reach.

"The one that ran us over," said Josh, biting into the cake so hard that the buttercream filling squidged out of the far side.

"Hang on – you've just seen her?" asked Aiden.

Josh nodded.

"That's weird because I saw her too. On the way here. She was at the Three Witches on the moor. Talking to someone – telling them to keep quiet."

"Definitely the same woman?" asked Ava.

Both the boys nodded.

"I'd know her anywhere," said Josh. "She was like Mrs Andrews – the PE teacher with sticky-out teeth and nail varnish."

"Uh?" said Ava.

"Oh, you know, all shiny and bags and make-up and stuff." Josh waved his arms around, vaguely describing big hair. "And high heels – very high heels."

"How long ago?"

"Oh." Josh shook his head from side to side. "Minutes – I took a shortcut, but she took the path, still carrying the bag."

"Do you think she was doing something … criminal?" asked Aiden.

"I dunno," said Josh. "But it was a really odd place to leave a bag."

"There must be something important inside it," said Ava, suddenly finding her brother interesting rather than irritating, "that someone else wants."

Aiden dropped Bella's lead to stand on the bench and scour the car park. "There it is – her car. It's over in the shady bit by the gift shop."

"So she's still here, somewhere," said Ava.

"I'm going to go and look in the car," said Josh, stuffing a second slab of cake into his mouth.

"No! Josh – don't! Wait!" shouted Ava, but he was already running towards the car park followed by Bella, her lead bouncing behind her. "Watch out for Bella, idiot!" she shouted across the people milling through the courtyard. A woman turned round and stared, and Ava suddenly found her sandwich very interesting.

Chloe wandered the gardens, searching for the toilets. A sign with a cup and saucer on it sent her past an old red telephone box and along a path that was completely overhung with wet grasses and big white daisies.

There was no way she was going to wade through it, but if she could just squeeze through the gap at the back of the telephone box… Just then, she heard muffled talking.

"I'm here," said a woman's voice. "Yes, at the Arrowhead Moor House phone box. No mobile phone signal in this hideous wilderness."

Chloe froze, listening.

"No, this wretched boy tried to give it back to me. Yes, I know – so I've still got it."

Chloe peered through the side of the box. Red shoes. And that voice. It was the woman who'd nearly run them over earlier, wasn't it? In the red car?

"So what do you want to do about it?" snapped the woman.

The end of Chloe's nose began to itch. Oh no, not hay fever, not already. She pressed her finger against her top lip like Grandpa had taught her to stop the sneeze.

"Well, I'm not sure. Is it easy to find?" The woman was sort of hissing down the phone as if she didn't want to be heard, so of course Chloe strained to hear every word.

"Yes, so, right out of the drive, I got that. And then left at the barn to the standing stones. Mmm. Yes, I see. Right. I'll leave it there in … twenty-five minutes? OK? And what about your part of the deal?"

The woman paused, listening.

"Where we agreed? You leave that while I leave yours. But I can't drive there. So you'll have to wait for a confirmation call. And I might have to find another call box." The woman's mac squeaked against the glass. "And what about the rest of the deal?"

There was a pause. "I don't know it, but… Yes, I do – there's a garden there… The Japanese one?

With ponds?" Another pause. "In the temple? Or the icehouse? Oh, yes. I get it."

Another pause. "Eleven o'clock tomorrow."

The woman listened. Chloe listened to the woman listening.

"No, we absolutely mustn't meet. Of course I understand the need for discretion – I'm not an idiot."

The phone clanked as the woman ended the call and then she began to walk fast. Her heels clicked on the path as she headed away, and Chloe crawled out from her hidey-hole behind the phone box, dying to share what she'd just found out.

CHAPTER 5

Keeping low, Chloe followed the woman through the gardens. The woman had a large black zippered holdall hanging from her shoulder.

Chloe ran back to the picnic area. Ava was standing alert, Aiden was trying to persuade Bella to sit in his bike basket, and Josh was fiddling with his shoelace. Ava saw Chloe and tilted her head towards the woman who was walking through the car park. Surprised, Chloe nodded in agreement. Their picnic had been packed away, and as she reached her cousins they mounted their bikes.

"C'mon," said Ava, holding out Chloe's bike.

"I think," said Chloe, shouting at their disappearing backs, "that I might know where she's going."

They kept the sports car in sight for about two minutes before the woman revved the engine and shot off over the moor. They pedalled madly for another minute before running out of breath.

"We've lost her," said Josh. "Now what?"

Aiden stood on his pedals, panting, watching the car until it vanished round a bend.

Ava flopped over her handlebars. "You said you knew where she was going?"

"I did." Chloe heaved in a lungful of air. "She rang someone from the old call box back there, and said something about standing stones. Are there some near here?"

"Map?" said Ava.

Everyone looked to Aiden, who hurriedly pulled the map from his backpack and spread it across his bike seat. "Here's Arrowhead Moor House. We're here…" He pointed. "But see here – the Old Maidens. The stone circle, remember? We had a picnic there once."

"When Josh fell in a bog?" asked Ava.

"I didn't really fall in a bog," protested Josh. "I just put my foot in some mud. Anyway, Ava, you got stung by a bee and turned into a giant cross balloon."

"What?" said Ava.

"Yes, when Josh fell in a bog, and someone got stung by something," said Aiden. "Anyway, they're pretty remote. If you wanted to meet in secret, it would be a good place. If we take this bridlepath It'll only take us about twenty minutes of cycling."

"That long?" said Chloe, sighing and looking down at her feet. Her flip-flops had worn a massive blister between her toes on one foot and the other was just sore.

Ava had been thinking. "For your information, Josh, it was a wasp."

"Plan?" asked Josh, ignoring his sister. "Get there and spring a surprise? We could dig into fox holes and surround them, or—"

"Or we could go home," said Chloe, examining her blister.

"What? And leave her to go around hanging

bags in trees?" said Josh. "I mean, that's, like, so suspicious. Why would you go around hanging bags in trees?"

Ava frowned at her brother. "It's not actually against the law."

"Anyone got a plaster?" asked Chloe.

Very slowly, Aiden looked from Josh to Chloe. "I think the rest of us want to go and see. Can you keep going?"

"Yes, course," said Chloe, crossing her fingers behind her back. "I'm fine."

CHAPTER 6

It was only a couple of miles of a lumpy bumpy track, and the rain held off while they cycled. Josh stopped at every turning, but Aiden pointed to the left each time.

They passed a barn and, away to the left, saw a ring of standing stones. The Old Maidens.

"Yay!" shouted Josh, and he shot off, crashing through bracken and gorse all the way to the stone circle. Bella leaped out of Aiden's basket and gave chase, barking all the way.

Ava and the others followed more cautiously,

pushing their bikes along the rabbit-nibbled paths until they reached the stones.

While Josh stamped around, looking at tyre tracks and writing things in his notebook, Chloe examined her feet and Ava checked for signs of anything hidden near the small gravel car park, just in case.

"No bag," she said.

With Bella trotting at his heels Aiden wandered out of the circle and down to another prehistoric feature that rose from the cropped grass like a giant rabbit warren. It was a long barrow, an ancient series of underground tombs accessed by a low doorway at one end. As he bent to peer into the darkness, he wondered how much it had changed in two thousand years. It might once have had a few more trees round about, he supposed, but the yellow broom must have flowered and the gorse and the bees probably hadn't changed. It was an ancient landscape. As his eyes adjusted to the black interior of the barrow he shuffled forward between the stones. There wasn't much here except for a few old candle stubs left by walkers.

Bella galloped in, sneezed, and immediately galloped out again.

There was no bag.

Aiden shivered, spooked by the darkness. Straightening up, he walked back to the circle. The others were sitting on a large flat stone to one side. Chloe was cutting an apple into four. Josh was licking the tinfoil that had been wrapped around the chicken.

"Anything down there?" asked Ava.

"Just the long barrow. No bag in it," said Aiden. "No anything. Perhaps Chloe got it wrong."

"Perhaps I did," said Chloe, reddening.

The sun broke properly through the cloud and fell on his face, hot and bright. The breeze had dropped. He closed his eyes for a moment and listened. No sheep, no cars. Just distant birds.

Suddenly the roar of an engine shattered the peace and apparently out of nowhere a small open-top red car screeched into the car park.

"Hide!" hissed Josh.

"Too late," said Ava. "Stay here."

The door of the car creaked open and the woman stepped out. She'd abandoned the mac and wore a neat grey jacket and skirt. Brushing her skirt flat, the woman leaned into the back of the car and reached for something. Then she paused, turned and looked at the cousins.

"Keep eating. Act normal," muttered Ava, trying not to stare at the woman.

"Hey," said Chloe to Josh. "You've eaten all the Scotch eggs."

"So? You don't even like them," said Josh, chucking a piece of tinfoil at Chloe. "Anyway, it was Bella."

"Oh my god! Cut it out, you two!" said Ava, slightly too loud.

The woman wandered over to them. Aiden noticed the bag hanging heavy on her shoulder. It was a large zipped black holdall. The kind of thing his dad took to the gym. Josh's eyes widened.

"Hello, kids," said the woman. "Nice lunch."

"Thanks. Yes," said Aiden, "it is." He couldn't think of anything else to say. He wanted to say "What's in the bag?" and had to practically bite his tongue to stop the words coming out.

Bella, who had been rummaging in the gorse, trotted back and sat staring up at the woman, her tongue hanging out, her head tilted to one side.

"Don't I…?" the woman began, then she looked at them in turn, her gaze settling on Josh.

"Have you got any plasters?" asked Chloe, holding her hand above her eyes and peering up at the woman.

"Pardon?"

"I've got a blister on my foot from my flip-flops. I wondered if you had any plasters? Please."

"Oh yes – her foot's a real problem," said Ava.

In an awkward silence the woman leaned forward and slipped the heavy holdall from her shoulder. "Let me see," she said, checking the much smaller shoulder bag she was carrying. "Oh yes," she said, handing one over to Chloe. "Here."

"Thank you," said Chloe. "Can you help me get the wrapper off, please?" She handed it back to her and nodded at Josh, who leaned away from the picnic and laid himself on the grass, his arms spread wide. His hand was almost touching the holdall.

The woman tutted and pulled a pair of pointy glasses out of her shoulder bag. "Um…" She put them on and fiddled with the plaster.

Josh wriggled his fingers up to the zip on the holdall.

"There!" said the woman, handing the opened plaster to Chloe and swinging round to grab the handle of the holdall. Josh only just had time to whip himself back into a sitting position.

"Bye then," said the woman and she wandered around the circle, stopping for a long time in front of the bronze plaque that described the history of the stones.

"Keep going," hissed Aiden, reaching across for a sandwich he didn't really want.

Ignoring the warning, Josh stood up and wandered back to his bike, rolling it across the circle towards the barrow. He knelt and fiddled with the brakes.

Aiden glared at him. It was far too obvious, but luckily the woman was having more difficulty trying to look normal, her heels sinking into the soft peaty turf, the bag heavy on her shoulder. Ever so slowly, she wandered out of the circle and down towards the barrow until she was out of view.

Aiden rose to his feet and crept across the circle. From here he could see down to the barrow entrance. The woman stood in the doorway, her back towards them. She was obviously struggling to see into the dark interior.

Aiden slunk back and sat with Ava and Chloe, all three trying to look utterly uninterested.

Josh, however, tiptoed even further forward until he was skulking behind the nearest of the standing stones, peering down towards the barrow and hissing things back to the others. Bella trotted along to sit beside him. "She's in there," he whispered.

"Shh," said Ava.

"She's putting it down."

Aiden glared at Josh and put his finger to his lips.

Suddenly Josh launched himself across the turf, scrabbling to reach them. A second later the woman appeared at the top of the path. This time with no bag and a tight smile on her red lips.

"Well," she said, looking at them doubtfully as if she'd just remembered where she'd seen Josh. "See you around."

"Yes," mumbled Chloe, and the others chimed in with feeble responses.

They waited.

Aiden stood and stretched, letting his eyes pass

over the car park. The woman was now standing by her car, looking back towards the cousins.

Aiden waved at her and then leaned down. "I think we should pack this lot up and look as if we're heading out. She's watching."

"Can't we…?" Josh nodded towards the long barrow.

"In a minute," said Ava.

Slowly the four cousins gathered their belongings, before picking up their bikes and wandering across the stone circle towards the lane.

The woman clambered into her car. Ava clambered on to her bike.

The woman started the engine. Josh pedalled – once, twice.

The woman drove slowly away, and the cousins pedalled very slowly after her, Bella cantering along the road.

When the red car disappeared over the top of the hill all four of them stopped, waited, then turned, pedalling frantically back towards the standing stones.

Ava was the first to abandon her bike in a bush, racing down towards the long barrow and stopping in the doorway blinking. Bella followed, barking and dancing as if this was the best game.

After hiding their bikes, the other three charged in behind her, but Chloe hesitated in the doorway. "It's very dark," she said.

None of them answered. Instead they crept down the narrow stone tunnel, bent at the waist.

"Can't see anything," said Ava.

"Ow!" yelped Josh. "My head!"

The barrow smelled of dead animals. And cold stone and wee.

Aiden switched on the screen of his phone and a dim light revealed the dripping ceiling of the barrow. It stretched ahead of them into a low dark cavern. There were stone built alcoves on either side big enough for a crouched person.

"Creepy," said Ava.

"'S a grave," said Aiden.

"Did they used to bury people in here?" asked Josh, examining the walls.

"In jars," said his sister.

"Ugh!" said Josh.

"I don't like it," said Chloe from the doorway.

"It's a very old grave," said Aiden. "Thousands

of years since anyone got buried in here."

"Still don't like it."

"Where's the bag?" said Josh.

All three of them were getting in each other's way. Ava switched on her phone and shone it at the roof, the walls and finally at the ground. There, tucked into the bottom of the wall, lay the holdall.

"Yay!" crowed Josh. "Here – let me——"

"Shh! There's someone coming," hissed Chloe, and she rushed into the barrow, shoving her way past Josh and towards the damp back of the cavern.

Footsteps thumped on the turf alongside the barrow and all four cousins scuttled into the furthest darkness. Bella remained at the entrance.

"Bella. Here," whispered Josh, but she wagged her tail and stood firm outside, looking up towards the path.

"Bella!"

"Shh," said Ava.

Aiden, who was nearest the entrance, waddled forward and grabbed Bella's collar, dragging her with him into the barrow. She let out a protesting yelp.

"Shh, Bella," he muttered, hugging her to his

chest. He could hear his heart pounding and Bella's breathing sounded far too loud. He wondered if anyone else could hear it.

Something wet moved against the back of his neck and he jumped, banging his head on the low ceiling. Slowly he reached round to find a snail investigating his hair.

Letting out a silent scream, he placed it on the floor of the cavern and shuffled even further back against the wall. He swallowed. He and Bella weren't really hidden.

The footsteps got closer and then Aiden saw a pair of booted feet and jeans in the light of the entrance.

"Got a torch?" said a voice.

Torch? Oh no!

"Shh," hissed Ava somewhere at the back of the barrow.

"Hang on a mo," said another voice. The boots stepped away from the entrance, presumably to fiddle about with a phone.

Aiden seized the moment. So silently he could almost hear the bones move in his shoulders, he clamped Bella under his arm and rolled the black bag as close to the entrance as he dared. Bella let out the tiniest whine, and Aiden clamped his hand round the end of her nose.

"Shh," he whispered, scuttling back into the dark of the cavern and jamming himself into the tiny alcove beside Chloe. He pulled his sweatshirt down over Bella's pale fur, willing her to keep quiet, but she scrabbled against him, scratching at his chest until her head popped out of the top.

A shaft of bright light bounced off the wall opposite, just catching the toe of Josh's shoe and resting on a pile of small bones lying on the packed-earth floor. Aiden closed his eyes, waiting for the moment when they were spotted.

"There it is!" said the second voice. "Over there!"

Aiden opened one eye.

"Proper Bronze Age thing this," said the first voice, the man with the boots. "If we had a bit of time, I'd take a look around."

"Well, we haven't," said the second, Scottish voice. "I'll just take a look at the bag, if I may."

Aiden opened his other eye.

Feet shuffled on the floor of the cavern and the light bounced back and forth, catching Josh's shoe and Ava's elbow. They both eased back into the shadows.

Aiden stared at the half-lit pile of bones. A rabbit?

From behind him came a strange clacking sound. Chloe's teeth? He nudged her and she let out something that might have been half a giggle or perhaps a whole sob.

His leg began to itch.

Bella licked his face. His eyes watered, and his glasses began to steam up. Brilliant. Now he couldn't even see properly.

There was the sound of a zip being yanked open down the length of the bag and then an intake of breath.

Aiden and Chloe risked leaning forward together.

Torchlight lit the entrance to the barrow and bounced up towards the men's faces. Through his steamy specs Aiden took in their fuzzy silhouettes before his eyes fell on the contents of the bag.

"Wow," said the Scottish man.

"Forty grand," said the other one.

Even with the fog Aiden could see purple – banknote purple. Next to him Chloe let out a tiny squeak.

"What was that?" One of the men shone the torch straight down into the barrow and Aiden and Chloe sprang back. To his right Aiden noticed that there was a tiny gap in the stones and he peered through to the entrance, hoping desperately that the men hadn't seen them.

The torchlight bounced around the chamber for a moment longer before the Scottish man spoke. "'S probl'y nothing, but let's not hang about, eh?" But the men still stared into the open bag and Aiden stayed in the darkness, staring at them through the tiny chink in the stones. One wore a yellow jacket with red stripes down the sleeves. The other wore black from top to bottom.

"She's done her half of the bargain," said Forty Grand eventually. "Hope our half is still there."

Scottish Man laughed. "I suppose some busybody might have decided to borrow it," he said. "I mean, they'll have a bit of a surprise when they sit down expecting a good read!"

"Yeah," said Forty Grand, sounding a little irritated. "Not in the original script. Stupid idea if you ask me. Anyway…" There was the sound of the zip being closed. "Let's go and wait to hear about part two." One of them dragged the bag across the floor and the torchlight disappeared. Then there was silence. The sound of water dripping through the stones. A crow.

The cousins sat in the dark, listening.

Then Bella burst out of the top of Aiden's sweatshirt and charged over to sniff at where the men had been.

It was another minute before Josh stepped out from behind Ava and headed for the entrance. "C'mon, what are we waiting for?"

CHAPTER 7

"Where do you think they were going?" shouted Josh, scribbling something in his notebook.

"Somewhere with books?" said Aiden.

"Yeah, I got that. A library? There's one in Drake's Bay," said Ava.

"There are the phone-box ones," said Josh. "That one in Ash Bottom has comics."

"Gotta be somewhere close. Oh my god – yuck!" said Ava, pulling a cobweb out of her hair.

"Think," said Aiden, yanking his bike up out of the long grass beside the standing stones. "They were putting whatever it was in a book somewhere else, while she was dumping the bag here."

"Hang on a minute," said Chloe, trying desperately to remember what she'd heard. "It's not on a road – I'm sure she said that she couldn't get there by car."

"You'd definitely need a road if you were moving a bunch of sheep," said Josh.

"There's one at Damsel Bradley," said Aiden. "By the old church. You can't take a car. You have to park in the village car park – miles out. That must be it." Swinging his leg over the crossbar, Aiden began to pedal away.

"I still don't get this," said Josh, climbing on to his bike. "What's it got to do with the stolen sheep?"

"I don't think it's got anything to do with the stolen sheep," said his sister, starting to pedal.

"Don't you think we should call the police?" shouted Chloe, climbing on to her bike and trying to catch up with the others. As she watched the back of Josh's bike vanish over a dip in the road she found herself wishing that the police were dealing with this, and also that she had something other than flip-flops to wear.

It took a few minutes to get to Damsel Bradley, and as they shot past the car park Ava noted that the red car was already parked there. She kept her eye out for the woman, but didn't see her until they were nearly at the heart of the village, where she was reading a noticeboard. Damsel Bradley was a tiny, very touristy village with a single pub, a shop and a huge walled garden that took up most of the centre. An ice-cream van stood in the tiny square, and Josh looked at it longingly.

"C'mon," said Ava.

She wiggled her bike along the edge of the crowd and headed up towards the church. She stayed well clear of the woman and led the others around the back of the church, where they leaned their bikes out of sight against a heap of stones.

"Quick," hissed Ava.

"No," said Chloe. "I'm just going to sit in the churchyard. It's too risky. She's almost up here."

"Suit yourself," said Josh, breaking into a run and legging it towards the phone box.

Chloe and Bella wandered into the churchyard and pretended to investigate the ancient stones.

Bella found a stick and began to chew.

Ava paused and looked back.

"Come on," Aiden said. "We've got about a minute."

The three of them ran to a red phone box and opened the door. Inside were ranks of books.

"How do we know…?" asked Aiden, holding the door open.

"Oh my god – this is hopeless," said Ava, biting her lip and searching the titles for anything helpful.

Josh started to pull books out at random, shaking them and jamming them back. Ava followed suit. Aiden stared at the books and reached out to take a single volume. "*Diamonds Are Forever*," he read aloud and flipped open the cover. The inside of the book had been carved out.

Back in the churchyard Chloe suddenly began to cough very loudly.

"That's a signal," said Ava, while Josh's nimble fingers whipped out a small black box that was nestled between the pages. He popped open the lid.

"Oh!" Inside were twelve shining stones. Despite the rain, despite the grey sky, light bounced off the facets of the stones and they seemed to glow against the blue velvet lining the box. "Wow!" he said. "Diamonds?"

"Quick, close it. Leave the diamonds," said Aiden. "And run."

They jammed the book back into the bookcase and threw themselves out of the door, falling over each other to plunge into the wet shrubbery beside the church.

"Twelve," whispered Josh. "There were twelve."

"Shh," said Ava, and then she put her hand over her mouth to stop a huge giggle coming out. "How did you know?" she asked Aiden. "The book I mean."

Aiden shook his head. "Luck – just luck."

Seconds later, shoes sounded on the stone path behind them and all three held their breath.

The shoes stopped and picked their way round to the phone box. The phone box creaked as someone opened the door and Ava sank further back into the bushes.

Something rustled in the bush behind her and Ava turned to see a dog's nose thrusting through the leaves. The dog snorted and snuffled and found Josh. Ava tried to push it away, but it was determined to lick Josh's face and incredibly he knelt in silence as it slathered his ears with drool.

"Come away, Bernie," said an elderly woman from behind them, and at last the dog was yanked off along the path.

Grimacing, Josh dragged his arm over his ears, leaving a silvery dog-goo trail over his sweatshirt sleeve.

The phone box creaked again, the footsteps faded, and Aiden tapped Ava on the arm. He pushed himself out of the bushes. Ava followed, Josh too, and they all crouched on the church path. The phone box was now on the other side of the hedge. They stayed where they were until the woman passed the end of the hedge. She had her back to them and was wearing the mac again. Her head was tilted down – she must have been looking inside the jewel box.

Her shoulders rose and fell – a sigh? – and she set off back towards the village. The three cousins followed her, but she veered towards Chloe in the churchyard. "You again!" she said.

Ava froze. The woman had no idea that they were behind her.

"Er – yes," said Chloe, her voice too high. "My cousins have gone to find me some more plasters."

"Whoops," Aiden said quietly, before melting away from Ava's side and running round towards the back of the church.

"How very strange," said the woman. "First you and your cousins are blocking the road as I drive over to that house…"

"Arrowhead Moor House," said Chloe.

Chloe was bright red. Ava gave her cousin a thumbs up.

"And then I come across one of you hiding in a field."

"Oh?" said Chloe.

"And then a moment later you're all having a picnic in a stone circle in the middle of the moor."

"Yes," said Chloe.

"And now here you are. I'd almost think you were following me."

"Well, we're not," said Chloe, smiling. Because of course they weren't strictly speaking *following* her. "We're just having a day out – doing…"

"Easter egg hunts," said Aiden, arriving behind Chloe, barely out of breath and clutching a box

49

of plasters and waving a piece of paper about an Easter egg hunt.

"Wow!" whispered Josh.

"Hmmmm," said the woman. And she stomped off down the cobbled path to the village, her high heels catching in the cracks at every step.

CHAPTER 8

"I really think we should tell the police," said Chloe as all four cousins sat on the wall of the churchyard sharing a bar of chocolate that Aiden had bought along with the plasters. "I mean, diamonds? Forty thousand pounds?"

"They might be stolen," said Ava, pulling out her phone and finding no signal. She put it away again. "But we haven't actually got any evidence. It could just be a really weird way of selling some diamonds."

"I think we should wait," said Aiden.

Chloe sighed. "What did they look like?" she asked. "The diamonds, I mean?"

Josh looked up from picking a scab on his knee. He considered saying "like raindrops" but in the end said, "Like diamonds. Sparkly and that." Then he sprang to his feet. "Anyway, last one back to the farm's a warthog." Cramming on his helmet he swung his leg over the crossbar of the bike and took off towards the centre of the village.

"Wait!" shouted Chloe behind him. "I'm coming." Her bike rattled as the two of them pedalled furiously down the hill until they must have been doing at least twenty-five miles an hour. Josh heard her panting alongside him and pushed harder until his legs were burning with the effort. They shot out of the village and past the car park, swerving wildly to avoid a woman with a child on the back of her bike.

"Go left!" shouted Chloe.

"No – right!" yelled Josh, and he leaned ever so slightly into the corner, neatly swinging into a lane that would eventually take them towards the sea.

"Josh!" protested Chloe. But he knew she'd follow.

For a few minutes the roads were empty, then they reached a crossroads and Josh screeched to a halt. There were three cars trying to come down from the moor and a stream of ten going the other way. Josh looked over them. "There they are!" he said, pointing. "The silver VW. The diamond men – that's them."

"You sure?" said Chloe.

"Definitely," said Josh. "One in a yellow jacket, red stripes on the sleeves; the other all in black. 'S all in my notebook."

The traffic jam began to unravel. "Ready?" said Josh, rolling forward as he prepared to chase the silver car a few metres ahead of them.

"Can't we just go home and call the police?" said Chloe, getting her pedal up so that she could push off. But it was too late. Josh had gone.

With a sigh Chloe followed him. He was, she supposed, heading sort of in the direction of the farm. It just wasn't the short way she'd have chosen. And they'd never be able to keep up with a car.

But their luck was in. The car in front of the silver VW was being driven by an elderly woman in a large hat, who took the road very carefully.

Josh and Chloe lagged behind, keeping out of sight of the silver VW. This worked well until the elderly woman swung off to the left.

Chloe watched as she turned, and slowed slightly. She was grateful that a light rain had started, which made it harder for anyone inside a car to see out.

But without the woman at the front the driver of the silver car sped up. Josh leaned flat over his handlebars and pinched his elbows in, like a real cyclist, picking up speed all the way.

There was no way Chloe was going to let Josh beat her, and soon they were charging unstoppably down from the moor. As she squeaked past potholes and ducked to avoid stray branches of brambles that stuck out from the hedges, she remembered the conversation she'd overheard. Both the men and the woman had talked about the second half of the deal. So they'd seen the first half. That meant there were probably more diamonds out there. But all thoughts went out of her head as they swept past the entrance of Clifftopper Farm, flying round the corners and descending madly towards Drake's Bay, both of them knowing every bend and every turn, both of them going dangerously fast. As they approached the church Chloe touched her brakes, ready to take the next bend towards the village, but the silver car didn't go on to the bay; instead it veered to the left, down Rosemary Lane and a tiny group of houses on the clifftop.

"Stop!" yelled Chloe, putting her feet down and feeling the soles of her flip-flops burn with the friction.

Josh squeezed his brakes and skidded to a halt thirty metres in front of her. "What?"

"We can't follow them there; it's too obvious. We'll watch from up here. We can see which house they go into."

Josh stood astride his bike, holding the handlebars. "What? Be more fun to follow them."

Chloe shook her head. "No – it'd be stupid. That woman's already got suspicious. She might ring them and tell them about us."

Josh glowered but stayed put. Chloe could feel his disappointment, but she wasn't going to go charging in and ruin everything. They needed to have a plan and Chloe knew from experience that Josh's plans tended to involve taking action and then thinking about it afterwards. Ignoring his sulk, Chloe watched the brake lights of the silver car glowing as it stopped outside the cottages.

For a moment no one got out, and then she saw the man with the yellow jacket climb out of the passenger seat and go through one of the little gardens at the front of the cottages. "There," said Chloe, pointing. "I think it's the one at the end."

Josh sighed. "Yeah," he said, pulling out his notebook and writing something. "You're probably right."

"So we've got more to tell the police now."

"S'pose so."

"After we've had something to eat back at the farm." She smiled and waited for his reaction.

She could almost feel his mood change. He rubbed his stomach, as if it was going to talk to him through his fingers. "Yay!" he said. "Beat you back to the yard."

CHAPTER 9

Aiden watched Josh and Chloe take off through the village. He grabbed his bike and thought about racing after them for a second before he heard Ava calling him back.

"No point," she said, zipping up her waterproof. "Josh's too fast on his bike. And he'll take a stupid route. He always does."

The light rain became heavier, dripping off the branches over their heads. Aiden swept water off his saddle and pulled the handlebars straight before freewheeling gently through the village. Stopping at the bottom by the bus stop, he took out the map and held it under the shelter. "If we go straight over the moor on this old track, we could cut miles off the ride. Chloe's probably right – we should call the police."

"C'mon then," said Ava, wrenching her bike round.

They left the village in the opposite direction to Josh and Chloe, and headed out along the moor. Bella trotted alongside, her fur already soaking. She no longer looked like a dog so much as a bath mat.

Ava pulled her waterproof closer and scrunched her nose up against the rain. She glanced back to Aiden. She knew he could barely see through his wet glasses and was just following her back.

"Look out for the track on our right," he shouted to her. "Soon."

She slowed. Even without specs it was hard to see where they were going, and the rain was beginning to creep in under the cuffs and round the neck of her waterproof. It was drifting across them in wet billows and every now and again they rode through deep puddles that threw water up over their legs. It was almost as if they were in a cloud, and it occurred to Ava that perhaps they were.

"Here," she said, and pulled off the lane. It was a rutty track, but it seemed to head off in a straight line over the moor. "This must be it."

Aiden pulled in behind her, took off his glasses and wiped them on something underneath his waterproof. He put them back on and, in the millisecond before they became wet, stared off down the track. "This looks right – I've done it in the sunshine before."

He didn't sound very sure, but Ava couldn't see any other track, so she swung her bike round and began to pedal. It didn't look particularly difficult, but it was harder than it seemed. It was very uneven, and she had to hang on to her handlebars as the bike twisted and pulled this way and that. She was so busy concentrating on staying on that she didn't look behind her until the mist became so thick that she could hardly see her hand in front of her face.

"Bella?" she called, her voice dead in the wet air. "Bella?"

A crow called in the distance and she put her feet down and stopped. "Aiden?" she said.

She turned. She couldn't see Aiden. She couldn't

see anything. "Aiden?"

There was no reply.

Looking down, she wondered if she'd actually stayed on the track, because now there seemed to be grass beneath her wheels and she couldn't see any sign of the gravel strip that she'd been following.

"Aiden! Where are you?" she yelled. And then she listened.

Silence.

She was on the moor, lost, with the cloud coming down.

"Oh. My. God. Aiden?" Her voice bounced off the mist.

The crow cawed again, but otherwise the moor was scarily empty.

"Bella?" There was no reassuring bark. Nothing.

"Don't panic," she said to herself.

The first thing she needed to do was establish where the track was. Or was it to work out which way was north? Would that help? She stared into the cloud. The sun should be in the south about now, but it was impossible to work out where the light was coming from. Reaching into her jeans she took out her phone and switched it on. No signal.

"Oh, please!" she said, and tried switching it off and then on again. Just in case.

Nothing.

Ava stood with her hands on the handlebars, listening to the rain brushing her waterproof. Chewing her lip, she tried to imagine what had happened to Aiden. He had definitely been behind her. So could she work out which way she'd come from?

Turning the bike round, she examined the turf. Water droplets clung to the stubby grass, except for one line where they didn't. "Yesss." That must be her bike track. Where her tyres had run through the grass, the water had been squashed and it showed green rather than silvery.

Clambering back on to her bike she began to pedal slowly back over the soft ground, keeping the line in sight. After a couple of minutes the line disappeared, but she saw the gravel track.

Ava stopped. "Oh." She breathed out slowly.

She could still only see a few metres, but it was obvious where she'd drifted off, going the wrong way round a large tussock at the side of the path, while the track snaked away to the right.

She heard the crow call again – or was it a crow? And again.

And was that a bark?

The sound came from somewhere further down the track. Was it possible that she'd veered off to the left and Aiden had pedalled straight on? He wouldn't have been able to see where he was going. She glanced down at her green jacket. It wasn't especially bright. It wouldn't show up much in the mist, particularly if Aiden's glasses were wet.

She pushed the bike along the track, keeping the tussock on her left this time and peering down in case there was any sign of Aiden's tyre marks. The ground rose and fell and the whole track began to tip downhill. Stopping, she listened to the misty rain falling on her waterproof and all the leaves.

There was that crow again.

"Aiden!" she shouted.

Her voice didn't really travel, but Aiden couldn't have gone far. They'd only been apart about ten minutes.

"Aiden!" she screamed, pulling her hood off so that she could hear.

"Ava!"

And barking. Bella barking.

"Where are you?" She stared into the rain.

"Here!"

She pushed the bike down the track and stopped. "Where?"

"Here!"

His voice was much louder this time. Staying on the track, she wandered down a little further, listening.

"I'm stuck!" he shouted. "Help!"

CHAPTER 10

"Stuck in what?"

"In a bog," came the reply.

Ava moved closer to his voice and scoured the track for any sign of him. "Which side?" she asked, no longer needing to shout.

"I think I may be on the right," he called, and at that moment she saw Bella, a paler blob in the white, and behind her something waving.

"Oh my god, Aiden," she said, spotting him. "You complete idiot."

He appeared to be waist deep in grass, but she

knew from Josh falling in one a couple of years ago that bogs were often invisible. They looked like large grassy tussocks, but beneath them the ground simply disappeared. She also knew that the more you struggled, the deeper you got.

"Where does it start?" she asked, standing back from the grass on the definitely solid gravel.

"Quite a long way out," said Aiden. "I am an idiot – I should have seen it."

"Yeah, but the fog," she replied, lying down and crawling forward, pushing the ground experimentally.

Alongside her, Bella sniffed and then let out a little yelp. "You know this is a bog, don't you?" said Ava. Bella shuffled and stood back from the grass.

"My bike's underneath me," said Aiden. "I rode it straight in. I'm dead glad to see you, Ava. I thought you'd never hear me."

Ava didn't say anything. She was trying to think of the best way to get him out.

"Does your phone work up here?" he asked.

Ava shook her head. "Going to have to work this out ourselves."

"Try pulling me out with your bike?" Aiden said.

Now that she was close she could see that Aiden's glasses were completely obscured. He really couldn't see a thing. But he was staying amazingly calm considering he was effectively blind and waist deep in a bog. "I haven't got a rope or anything to tow you with."

"Not like that," he said. "If you put it flat on the bog and pulled from your end, I could hang on to the other end and maybe you could tug me out."

"What about your bike?"

"If I can, I'll hook my knee round the crossbar. It's not very heavy…"

"Seriously?"

Ava lay her bike flat across the bog, pointing the front wheel towards Aiden. The wheel reached him easily and he took it in both hands.

She sat on the ground and, bracing her feet against a lump of grass, Ava took the back wheel in both hands and began to pull.

Bella raced around behind her, a sort of doggy encouragement.

"Slow," said Aiden.

Ava tried to keep pulling, but nothing seemed to be moving except Aiden's arms, which appeared to be getting longer. "Think I need to try plan B," she said.

"What's plan B?" asked Aiden, looking more than slightly worried.

"Going to try standing," she said, scrambling to her feet. "I'll be pulling the weight of the bike and you, but this isn't working."

"And what if that doesn't work?" said Aiden.

"We'll have to try plan C."

"Which is?"

"I dunno yet."

CHAPTER 11

"Can we use the phone, please?" asked Chloe as she sat on the steps of the barn and pulled back the plaster that covered her blisters.

Josh prodded her.

"What?" She glanced up at him, frowning.

Grandma looked from Chloe to Josh. "Is it important?"

"Nah," said Josh. "Don't worry. It's just some people acting suspiciously. Chloe wanted to ring the police."

Grandma sat back, laughing. "Oh, you are a

hoot, Josh – your stories. They do make me laugh. And where were these suspicious people?"

"At the barrow on the moor," said Josh. "And the phone box in Damsel thingy."

Grandma continued to laugh and rose to her feet. "Anyway, dears, while you're waiting for the others, why not have a scone? They're supposed to be for the film club, but I think you could sneak one or two without annoying your grandfather." She set off towards the house.

Chloe looked across at Josh. "Why shouldn't I call the police?"

Josh shrugged. "It's more fun if we don't tell anyone," he said. "Anyway, I just did, and she didn't believe me, so we need to get more evidence before we try to tell anyone else."

Chloe sniffed the heavenly scent coming from the kitchen and nodded.

"So, Grandpa, what happens if you eat the cream and jam without the scones?" asked Josh, leaning over the huge pot of cream in the middle of the table.

Grandpa smiled and flapped Josh away. "Then

the film club will have nothing to eat when they come round to discuss the summer programme."

"We could maybe get you some more cream?" said Chloe, watching the scones rising in the oven.

"No need for that," said Grandpa, reaching into the fridge. "I've got plenty of jam, plenty of cream and, actually, plenty of scones. BUT –" he said, as Josh's hands shot forward – "you can have two each when I take them out, and absolutely no more. OK?"

Chloe nodded, and glanced across at Josh, who was also nodding but had his fingers crossed behind his back. She poked him and he glared at her before laughing.

"Promise, Grandpa," he said, this time without his fingers crossed.

As Grandpa took the first batch of golden scones out of the oven, Grandma switched on the radio.

Chloe watched Grandpa's old brown hands land the tray of scones on a large mat. She watched as he flicked each scone on to a wire rack and she realised that she was *really* hungry.

"*In local news, a hunt is on across the Dragon Peninsula for several ewes taken from a farm last night. If you have any information, please call…"*

As steam rose from the scones Chloe listened to the news report. *"And the headlines again. Police in the London area are hunting for a gang of jewel thieves. The thieves, who broke into safety deposit boxes at Hatchard's Bank early on Tuesday morning, are believed to have taken the sixty diamonds that make up the famous Eliza Necklace – once owned by Queen Victoria and presented to her by Princess Eliza of Russia in 1851. The necklace had been awaiting repair…"*

Chloe stopped, her hand outstretched. She and Josh exchanged looks. Suddenly the scones seemed less delicious.

"The largest of the diamonds, known as the Well of Beauty, measures more than five centimetres across and sits at the heart of the necklace. Scotland Yard are interested in interviewing anyone with any information. And the weather – further rain is expected…"

Chloe took a scone and split it. As the steam rose she took a teaspoon of cream and spread it across both halves before landing a small splodge of jam in the middle.

Jewels.

Diamonds.

The Eliza Necklace.

The second half of the deal.

"Wow," said Josh next to her.

"Exactly," said Chloe, eating her scone in three scalding bites. "I think we need to talk."

"Now?" he said.

"Yup!"

"Thanks, Grandpa," they chorused, rushing from the table.

"Really?" said Grandpa, whisking away their plates. "You've had enough?"

"They were lovely, Grandpa," said Chloe, pausing in the doorway, "delicious, and I'd love to have more, but there's something—"

"We've got to do!" yelled Josh, grabbing her elbow and yanking her back out into the rain.

CHAPTER 12

Aiden trusted Ava. He trusted her completely. It was just that so far plan A and plan B weren't working very well.

"OK – two more goes, and then I think I'll go for help."

"Good," said Aiden.

He didn't want to make a fuss, but he was beginning to wonder what had happened to his legs. They'd gone completely numb, and where earlier he'd been able to feel the crossbar of the bike with his foot, it seemed to have gone. He wasn't even sure if he was moving his foot any more. Leaning forward, he felt the water slosh up around his armpits. He'd sunk lower in the bog, but he was so cold the water seemed almost warm. Almost nice. He could just fall asleep.

"OK," said Ava, turning the bike round the other way. "Hang on to the crossbar; I'm going to pull the saddle. Might work better than the wheels."

Aiden hoped she was right. He'd worked out that it would take her half an hour to pedal all the way uphill to the village, then probably another half an hour to come back with a search party – and that was if she could even find her way back to him in this fog. He wasn't sure he could hang on for that long.

Although his fingers were so cold he could barely feel them, he clamped them round the crossbar. It was definitely easier to hold than a wheel. Holding the other end of the bike, Ava was balanced on a grassy lump, and it occurred to him that in a couple of minutes they might both be stuck in the bog. And then who would rescue them?

"One, two, three – go!"

Bella danced and barked as Ava pulled.

Aiden gripped as hard as he could and he leaned forward, willing himself out of the bog. "Nearly," he muttered. "Just…"

"Yup," she whispered, closing her eyes and putting in another massive effort.

Squooooooooch. A long, low sucky sound came from the bog as it began to release him. Ava leaned backwards, pulling the bike right up over her chest, and Aiden scrabbled at the tussock to haul himself out. His arms were flailing, his legs almost useless. Looking down, he was amazed to see the bike following. Black and dripping with mud it rose from the water, jammed between his knees.

"Yay!" gasped Ava, falling backwards across the track.

Bella raced all the way round the bog, yelping.

Aiden couldn't speak. He was so relieved, so exhausted, that words escaped him. Instead he lay in a widening pool of black water, and was suddenly overtaken by shuddering as the cold ran through his whole body.

"Can you stand up?" asked Ava, staggering upright.

She leaned over and set Aiden's bike vertical,

kicking some lumps of mud and grass from the chain and shaking off some of the ooze.

"Think so." Aiden knelt, before lifting one leg, then the other. Tottering, he balanced on his dead legs. Pins and needles crept up his calves, and he had to stamp his feet to stop the combination of cramp and shivers that ran up and down them.

Ava peered at him. "Cycle? It's a long way to walk."

Aiden nodded and slung his leg over the saddle. He tried to pedal, surprised to find that after its ordeal the bike was still perfectly functional. "Yes," he said, still struggling to form words. "Yes. Bike."

CHAPTER 13

Ten minutes later, and all the while keeping an eye on the cottage at the clifftop, Chloe and Josh had established a pretty good tree house in the branches of one of the old apple trees that overlooked the bay. A pallet rescued from the beach last summer, draped with two blue tarpaulins and lined with feed sacks, made a fine viewing platform almost completely protected from the sea mist that came and went.

"I'll take the first watch," said Josh, climbing up into the den. "You can go and get supplies."

"I'm not getting supplies," said Chloe, passing him a milk crate that she had taken from the bike shed. "You can do that – you're the one that's always hungry."

"Aw," moaned Josh, sitting on the crate.

But Chloe wasn't going to give in. She climbed up into the tree and nestled alongside Josh, butting against him so that they could both sit on the crate and so that they could both see the cottages on the clifftop.

Rain dripped off the tarpaulins, but they were cosy inside. Never mind that they had got wet setting it all up and that their soggy waterproofs were lying in a pool at their feet.

While Josh looked down towards the sea, Chloe found herself glancing uphill towards the moor. She was desperate to share what they'd discovered about the diamonds and the theft with the others. She wanted them all to talk it through together, to design a proper strategy. She knew Josh would just race down and bash on the door of the cottage and demand the diamonds back, but they needed to be cleverer than that or they'd end up in trouble.

"Do you think the other two are all right?" she

asked, peering up the hill for the millionth time in the hope of seeing them.

"I've been wondering that," said Josh, stripping the bark from an apple twig. "I reckon… Oh, look!"

Bella galloped down into the farmyard, followed seconds later by two bikes: one shiny with Ava on top, the other grubby and black with a matching filthy person on top.

Chloe leaped down from the den and raced across the orchard. "Where have you two been? What happened?"

"The rain happened," said Ava.

"And a bog," said Aiden.

"And getting … lost," she said.

"And a rescue," he continued.

"We had scones," said Josh from the tree. "They were delicious."

Ava stuck her tongue out at him. "Well we didn't," she said.

"And," said Chloe, "we know where those diamonds are from and we know there are more."

"Good," said Aiden, peeling a long strand of grass from the mud streaks on his cheek. "But can I change my clothes first?"

While Chloe brought cushions from the conservatory, and Aiden had a shower and found two more milk crates, and Josh dug out the coconut drops that his mum had sent him with, Ava kept watch. No one came or went from the house on the clifftop and she began to wonder if the men had left, but she didn't think they could have done – not unless they'd sneaked off somewhere on foot, because the car was still parked outside the cottage. She shuffled across the pallet and peered round the corner towards Sunny Grange House. It stood on its own, a small house with a huge conservatory that was open to the public because it had once belonged to someone famous. They'd normally have visited this holiday, but it was closed for restoration. No. No one would escape that way; that road didn't really go anywhere, and anyway the men in the cottage wouldn't think anyone was watching them. They didn't need to be furtive.

Chloe threw some cushions in and ran back to get more, while Aiden and Josh squeezed in, and the three of them sat in the tree house listening to the rain pattering on the tarpaulins. Josh shifted and pushed against the lower of the two covers and a long string of water dropped past the opening, just missing Chloe, who was halfway up the tree. Out of breath, Chloe stuffed a final two cushions in through the entrance and threw herself in afterwards.

"Right—" said Josh.

"The two men," interrupted Chloe, "are down there, as you—"

"The men that must actually have stolen the jewels that is," butted in Josh.

"Stolen?" said Aiden. "How do you know that?"

"Because of the radio," said Chloe. "And the woman—"

"Wait," said Ava, holding up her hands. "Start at the beginning."

"So," said Chloe, "turns out that this really—"

"Really—" said Josh.

"*Really*—" said Chloe.

"Valuable necklace was stolen from a bank in London," finished Josh.

"We never saw a necklace," said Ava.

"It was in bits – just the diamonds, on their own. It'd been taken apart for cleaning or mending or something," said Josh.

"There are sixty of them altogether," said Chloe. "Plus this huge one called the well of something – and it used to be Queen Victoria's."

"It's called the Eliza Necklace and it came from Persia."

"Russia," Chloe said, correcting Josh.

"Sixty? I don't get it," said Ava. "We saw twelve. How do we know it's the same necklace?"

Chloe and Josh both opened their mouths ready to speak. Chloe won. "When we were at Arrowhead Moor House I overheard the woman talking to someone on the phone." She pointed down the hill to the cottages. "To those two, I think, and she said something about discretion, and meeting up tomorrow for part two –" Chloe took a coconut drop – "at eleven, and, really importantly, when we were in the barrow the men also said *part two*."

"So…" said Ava, leaning forward.

"So we think that the twelve we found in the phone box are part one – you know, like a sign of quality – and that the woman in the red car—"

"With the money bag—" said Josh.

"Was buying those twelve," said Chloe, "to show

that she had the money – or something."

"And they were showing that they had the real thing." Josh looked pointedly at Ava and Aiden. "Real quality diamonds."

"Josh, what are you saying?" asked Ava.

Josh pointed to the clifftop cottage. "We're saying – aren't we, Chloe? – that the rest of the necklace, the rest of the diamonds, are down there – in that cottage."

"Including the well of whatnot?"

"Yes," laughed Chloe. "Including the well of whatchamacallit! Yes, the well of thingamabob in that cottage down there!"

CHAPTER 14

"Why don't we just get the police?" said Chloe.

"They won't believe us," said Josh. "Even Grandma wouldn't believe us."

"And because of the sheep," said Ava. "They're all running around after the stupid sheep."

"We can't really go down there with Grandpa Edward and just ask for the diamonds back, can we?" said Chloe.

"We're going to have to do something soon, though," said Aiden, staring at the cottage on the clifftop. "They could drive off at any time."

"Why don't we set up a diversion?" asked Josh. "I know – we could set fire to their car. That would get them out of the house really fast! Then we could steal back the diamonds. Done!" Josh mimed grabbing something from mid-air.

The other three just stared at him. Josh thought it was quite a good idea, but it was obvious that, as ever, Ava didn't.

"If eleven o'clock tomorrow is the end of the deal," continued Aiden, ignoring Josh, "then they'll definitely leave after that."

"So we capture them!" said Josh. "Yes!" He leaped out of the tree house and across the garden and fenced an apple tree with a bamboo cane. "Yes – we can spring a trap and drop a huge net on them from above. We could dig an enormous—"

"Oh my god, Josh. Get real. We need to get the diamonds back before eleven o'clock tomorrow," said Ava, cutting right through Josh's brilliant ideas and discarding them. "Where is the eleven o'clock thing, Chloe?"

Chloe scrumpled up her face with the effort of replaying the woman's words. She couldn't remember what she'd heard. "I just can't get it," she said in the end, looking disappointed.

Josh sighed, groaned and died dramatically on the wet grass, where Bella discovered him and began to lick his face with enthusiasm.

"Even if we can't catch them handing things over, we might be able to get the necklace back," said Aiden.

"Really?" said Chloe.

"What d'you think, Ava?" asked Aiden.

Ava raised an eyebrow and gazed down towards the clifftop cottages. "P'raps we could."

"How are you going to do that then?" asked Josh, clambering up the apple tree and hanging from the top branch. "You're never going to break into a house, are you? Are you?"

Ava glared at him and swept off towards the farmhouse.

Grandma and Grandpa's friends came and went, and the sun sank lower. Ava scoured her and Chloe's clothes until she found what she was looking for − a long-sleeved black sweatshirt and some black leggings. She finished the outfit off with black socks and black canvas shoes.

"What d'you reckon?" she asked Chloe.

"You look very – criminal," said her cousin, walking round her. "Do you think you can do it, though?"

Chloe looked doubtful, so Ava tried to sound confident. "Of course. Easy."

Aiden appeared at the door of their room. "Ready?"

Ava nodded.

"We'll all be there," he said. "But it's your thing."

"I know," she said, thinking that at least fifty per cent of her head was telling her not to do it. "C'mon, let's go."

She led the way down the stairs, the others following, and out through the garden, where the dusky light was enough for them to find the footpath that led over the field towards the sea. They'd decided not to take Bella. Or bikes. This way they could run over the fields if they had to. But Ava felt very slow putting one foot in front of the other instead of flying along the roads almost as fast as a car.

As they approached the little group of houses they fell to a crouch. Josh and Aiden slipped along the hedge to the gate and opened it a fraction so that they could escape through it quickly if they had to. The silver car still sat outside and Ava passed her hand over the bonnet. "Cold," she whispered to Chloe. "They haven't been out."

"They still have the necklace then."

Ava nodded.

Three wheelie bins stood in the lane and the two girls crouched behind them, waiting for the sky to go black. Here there was only one weak street light over by the cliff edge and the shadows were pleasingly murky. Inside the house someone switched on a light. It shone through the glass over the front door.

Ava crept forward, Chloe at her back, and they stopped by the fence that ran round the front garden. Between the gaps Ava could see in through the window. No one was in the dining room, which was lit by a broad band of light from the hallway. A table and four chairs stood neatly in the middle, and a sideboard with four bowls and a vase stood at the back. Over the fireplace was a large photo of Drake's Bay.

"Holiday cottage," mouthed Chloe.

Ava nodded. That would make it easier to search the house. It would be emptier.

As the darkness deepened she sat back on her heels and waited. No one came; no one left. The phone didn't ring. No one even seemed to come down the stairs.

Ava's heart pounded.

They waited.

CHAPTER 15

Meanwhile Aiden and Josh explored the back.

"I'll jump the fence," whispered Josh, and before Aiden could stop him he had vanished over the top.

"Ow!" Aiden heard from the other side. *Josh, you idiot*, he thought, and listened with his ear to the wood.

"Can't reach the handle," he heard Josh whisper.

Feeling the fence with his hands, Aiden headed towards the front of the house. Halfway along he found a gate that joined with the passage down the side of the house. Agonizingly slowly he lifted the latch.

Josh appeared in the gap and beckoned him through. "Shh," he whispered to Aiden, as if Aiden needed to be told.

In three paces they were over the tiny lawn and hidden behind two plastic garden chairs.

The curtains were drawn across a large pair of sliding doors, but as they crept further forward it became easier to see through the gap between them. It was the lounge. Two sofas and a huge TV. A coffee table with two mugs, and a rug. And a pair of feet resting on the coffee table.

"One," he whispered to Aiden, who nodded.

Without warning the door to their right opened. The kitchen door? A man stepped out on to the paved area and dropped a bag by the door. He didn't stop to look at anything, just went back inside and slammed the door shut. Josh and Aiden hadn't even had time to hide.

Josh breathed out. "Two," he whispered.

That was close, Aiden thought.

The light went out in the kitchen and moments later a second set of feet appeared on the coffee table. Someone flicked the remote control and the guide came up on the TV. There was a rumble of conversation and the man with the remote clicked down the options before choosing a film. One of the men got up and a toilet flushed. The light in the kitchen came on and then there was the steady rumble of a kettle. Cupboard doors opened and closed and then a few moments later two more mugs appeared on the coffee table alongside a packet of biscuits. The men seemed to settle to drinking tea and eating biscuits, and the film began.

"Tell Ava," said Aiden. "Now would be good."

"You tell her," said Josh, sitting back on the wet grass.

Resisting the impulse to say something really rude, Aiden crept off towards the far side of the house, back to the gate and Ava.

Ava was so sprung with nerves that when Aiden appeared round the side of the house she leaped in surprise. "Oh my god!" she squeaked.

"C'mon," he whispered. "They're watching TV."

Ava took a deep breath. "OK," she said.

She padded along the path and pushed the front-door handle down as slowly and steadily as she could. Leaning her shoulder against the door, she gave it a gentle shove, then tried pulling. Nothing happened. It was locked. She turned to Aiden and shrugged.

Aiden beckoned and led the way back round the house. On their way through the narrow passage one of them brushed against a bin lid.

Clang.

Ava froze, trying to control her breathing, and listened. She waited to hear a door open or someone shout. But nothing happened.

She let the air out of her lungs. The passage they were in was extra dark and the garden at the far end seemed flooded by bright moonlight. She could see Josh hiding behind the chair, the lights from the window, the gap in the curtains.

"Think the back door's open," whispered Aiden. "Two bedrooms upstairs. A loo downstairs. Probably a bathroom upstairs."

"Sure there are only two of them?" whispered Chloe.

"Yes," said Aiden. "Definitely."

"OK," said Ava. "I'm going in."

She crept to the door, turned the handle and felt the catch spring open. She pulled it as quietly as she could and stepped inside. The sounds immediately changed. The distant beating of the sea and the low chatter of the village turned to a rumbling TV and a distant boiler. The kitchen smelled of frying and she was horrified to see that the sink was full of dirty pots and pans. That meant that someone might come and do the washing up and it might be just as she was coming back out.

With the same care as she'd opened it she closed the door behind her and took three paces into the hallway. Her feet clicked on the wooden flooring as she passed the door to the lounge. It had a glass panel in the centre and the light shone through. She hoped no one could see her shadow pass on the other side.

Waiting for the noise of an action sequence on the television, she sped past the door and went on into the darkened dining room at the front of the house. Feeling sick with fear, she slid open the drawers of the sideboard. They were empty. She peered into the vase. It too was empty. She wanted to run, but she made herself check the cupboards. There didn't appear to be anything but some games. Agonisingly slowly she pulled out a box of Scrabble and slid off the elastic band that held the lid. It rattled and she paused, listening. All she could hear was the TV. So slowly she was barely moving, she prised the lid free. Scrabble pieces, of course, but she had had to see.

Leaving the dining room, she headed for the stairs. One by one she took the treads, her feet brushing the carpet and sounding really loud. She reached the top and hoped that the boards wouldn't creak.

The room at the front was easy. It was over the dining room, where there was no one underneath to hear her, so she took it first. A bed, a bedside table with nothing in it. A chest of drawers. The top drawer stuck immediately, and she had to shuffle it from side to side to get it to open. When she did she found it empty. It was the same with the other four. A suitcase stood by a long mirror and she wasted precious minutes trying to open the zips, finding each compartment still full of neatly folded clothing. Fingering her way past tidy piles of socks and pants, she checked the corners of the case. Nothing.

With shaking hands she closed the zips and placed the suitcase exactly where it had been. Stopping in the doorway, she took a deep breath, desperate to steady the rising panic that threatened to make her run for the kitchen door and safety.

She moved to the back bedroom, barely making contact with the floor. She worked as fast and as silently as possible and found nothing. Again there was a suitcase. More zips, more clothes. More compartments. She shook out the socks, patted the pockets of the jackets and prodded the sides.

No luck, she thought as she tiptoed back on to the landing.

The bathroom was small and had very few hiding places, although she tried the cistern and squeezed the toothpaste just in case.

Which left the downstairs toilet. And the lounge.

She paused at the top of the stairs.

Bang.

Someone had opened a door downstairs. She heard a tap go on – then off – followed by the rumble of the kettle.

Hesitating for a terrified moment, she retreated into the bathroom. Footsteps fell heavily in the hall and then, to Ava's horror, she heard feet on the stairs. Looking around, she grabbed the bath mat, threw it over her head and crouched under the basin. The footsteps reached the top of the stairs, paused, and then she heard someone go into the back bedroom and unzip the case.

Her mind ran through all the things she'd seen in the case and she hoped desperately that she'd put them back as they were.

The footsteps retreated to the landing. She held her breath, her heartbeat thudding in her ears, and she pulled her head lower and lower between her knees, willing her whole body to disappear into the floor. Then, when she thought she was going to explode, the footsteps began to descend the stairs. Slow and heavy, she heard them turn at the bottom, the kitchen door thump, some mugs clank together and then the lounge door. Voices rumbled and the TV took over again.

Ava breathed out, long and slow.

CHAPTER 16

In the garden, Chloe and the boys watched the lights go on and off as the man went upstairs. They waited, ready to cause a diversion, but the lights moved downstairs and there was no sign of trouble.

Chloe tried to work out where Ava was. She'd seen a shadow upstairs and then in the bathroom, but Ava had been in there for ages and really ought to be coming out. "What's the time?" she whispered to Aiden.

"Nine thirty," he replied. "She's been in there for half an hour."

"Too long," said Josh.

Silently Chloe agreed, and when both the men stood up and switched off the TV, she realised that they'd really run out of time.

"Diversion," muttered Aiden, but Chloe didn't need telling.

No longer worrying about secrecy, Chloe and Josh raced round to the front of the house. They hadn't planned anything, so they were going to have to make it up as they went along.

"Ow!" screamed Chloe. "Ow! Help!" she shouted, yelling in the direction of the house before suddenly realising that they might end up getting help from one of the other cottages, which would be no use at all. "Help!" She shoved Josh forward and mimed banging on the door.

"Help!" he shouted. "My sister's been – she's been … stung by a wasp!"

"What?" Chloe stopped moaning for a moment and stared at Josh. "Way too early in the year for wasps," she hissed, hopping about on one foot. "And they don't sting at night."

"A sleeping wasp in her sock!" yelled Josh.

"Ow!" yelled Chloe again. "I've been stung."

"Help!" Josh banged on the door again and Scottish Man pulled it open as he was still knocking. "We need some vinegar."

"'Aven't got any," he said, starting to close the door. He seemed half asleep; Chloe hoped he really was.

"We need it desperately," said Josh. "My brother, er, sister, she's allergic to wasps. She's been stung; she might die." Chloe saw the lie growing more complicated and hoped Josh wouldn't say anything too stupid.

"Try one of the other houses," the man said, glancing towards the lounge.

"What's going on?" The second man arrived behind him. This was Forty Grand. Seeing his face was scarier. Mean, scarred, battered. Like a real criminal.

Like a bearded rat, Chloe thought. Scottish Man looked much kinder, and he didn't look very kind.

"Kid's been stung by a bee," said Scottish Man.

"Get over it," said Forty Grand. "Hey! What's that?" He turned, looking behind him, and Chloe shot a glance past him to see Ava belting down the stairs and swinging round to run through the kitchen door. "Hey!"

Both men turned, leaving the front door wide open, and charged towards the kitchen.

"I'm off," said Josh and he raced for the fields.

Chloe hesitated. She stood on the path, trying to work out if there was anything she could do to slow the men down. And then she saw the car keys lying on the table in the hallway.

"Yes!" she cried, and grabbed them, jamming them into the back pocket of her jeans and speeding up to catch Josh. They ran straight over the stile and into the field.

As they raced through the wet grass Chloe heard the thundering footsteps of Aiden and Ava, who had charged round the side of the house and were now heading full pelt for the open gate.

"Quick!" Ava yelled, and all four ran in a line, skimming over the grass and down towards the dip in the field.

"Split!" shouted Aiden, and they separated.

Chloe ran up towards the top of the field where she knew there was a small gap. She squeezed herself between a fence post and the wall. On the other side cattle shuffled and breathed. "Hello, cows," she said, bending double and pushing through between their warm hides. Wet noses brushed her ears, but the animals stayed where they were and let her race through them. She thought of staying put, but decided it was better to get as far away from the clifftop cottages as possible. Tracking the hedge of this new field, she scrambled over a metal gate into the lane.

Just then the clouds drew back and revealed the moon. It lit the entire landscape. Chloe looked back to see the lights blazing in the clifftop cottage and the tall man stamping about in front of it. But there was no sign of the second man until a figure burst from a small group of trees and a second figure shot out in pursuit. The first person was Aiden, the second Forty Grand. Chloe watched, willing Aiden to escape. She knew he knew the fields really well – that he was the fastest runner of them all – but she wasn't sure he'd make it out of that field before his pursuer.

And it was dark, and he wore glasses.

She heard someone running in the lane and looked to the side. "Josh!" she said. "Look – Aiden."

They stood side by side, staring into the darkness

as Aiden ran back along the line of the fence.

"There's no way out down there; we're going to have to rescue him," said Chloe.

"How?" said Josh.

"I don't know. Let's run towards him. We'll think of something on the way."

CHAPTER 17

Aiden was running out of breath. All that time in the bog had tired him out and now, racing up and down the field in the dark, his legs felt like lead. But the man's breathing behind him kept him moving. Somewhere in this field was a stile, and on the other side a large ploughed field. The plough lines would be hard to run across, but he was hoping they'd be harder for the large man behind him. He swung back to his left – where was that stile?

Clang!

Something crashed over to the right. In the dark

it was difficult to see but it looked as if a load of large black things were flowing towards him.

Cows?

"Go – on!" he heard Josh cry and then thundering hooves.

It *was* cows. Brilliant.

Aiden raced up towards the gateway, dodging the cattle, and heard the yelp behind him of the man not dodging the cattle.

In the moonlit darkness it was hard to avoid the confusion, but he knew that if he kept to the left of the gateway, there was a pedestrian gate, and he'd be able to get through.

All around him the cows milled, thundering chaotically back and forth across the turf, bellowing and stamping. Wet noses lunged towards him and more than once he was flicked by a flying tail, and all the while his feet slipped on the wet grass.

"Here," he heard Chloe hiss. She was holding the side gate open and he threw himself through and followed her and Josh to the top of the field, where they scrambled over a collapsed piece of wall and stopped in the lane.

Aiden leaned over, resting his hands on his

knees while he gulped in breath. "Phew," he said. "Thanks. That was close."

Below they could hear cows mooing and the man shouting and the other man shouting too. They sounded a long way away. A safe distance.

"Will those cows get out?" he asked.

"No," said Chloe. "We checked that the gates were closed."

Aiden breathed deeply, filling his lungs with the cowy night air. He surveyed the fields. "But where's Ava?"

Ava was crouching in the back of a warm shed at Sunny Grange House, three hundred metres down the path from the clifftop cottages. She had heard the shouting, she had heard the running, but she stayed put because she didn't trust her legs to run as fast as they needed to. Searching that cottage had been so terrifying that her knees seemed to have given up. Even clambering over the small fence into this garden and running to the shed had been a trial, so she'd decided she'd wait until it all went silent before she set off again. Besides there was the strangest sound coming from next door.

Sort of sheepy.

*Baa*ing and shuffling, and that smell – like old woolly jumpers.

All of which was odd when you considered that she was hiding next door to an ornamental greenhouse in a garden that was open to the public three days a week.

Ava straightened her legs and shook the muscles of her thighs to stop them twitching.

Baaaaa!

Tiptoeing through the shed, Ava peered through the little window at the back that looked out into the conservatory. The old-woolly-jumpers smell became more intense and the rustle of animals moving around in the moonlight became more obvious.

She smiled to herself. "Oh my god, sheep – there you are!" she said. "All snug in the conservatory."

The sheep just shuffled and chewed and tore at the hay that had been left for them.

And then she remembered. The house was closed until May. Someone was supposed to be painting the greenhouses, not hiding sheep in them. Clever. They probably knew that no one would check it over the weekend.

Ava clicked her phone on. Midnight. All the running around had stopped. The only sounds came from the sheep.

Straightening herself up, she opened the door of the shed and stepped out into the velvety blackness.

CHAPTER 18

At breakfast the scrambled eggs and hot buttered toast disappeared at double speed, washed down with apple juice. Ava was there. She looked a little baggy-eyed but otherwise fine, and Josh wondered if she'd managed to get the diamonds. Last night, Chloe had made Ava noises in the bathroom and dropped wet towels all over the landing. They'd pretended that Ava had already gone to bed with a headache. But the truth was no one had seen her.

Catching her attention, Josh raised an eyebrow, but she ignored him and filled her glass with more juice. "Ava?" he asked.

This time she raised her index finger and pointed out towards the garden. "Garden," she mouthed.

"Another one of these, anyone?" said Grandpa, turning from the stove, a hash brown delicately balanced on his fish slice.

Josh held his plate forward, hopeful that the hash brown would land with him, but Chloe got it.

He tried not to look disappointed, but Grandpa must have seen it. "There'll be another one along in a moment, Josh."

Josh beamed.

"You're all very quiet this morning," said Grandma, coming in with Bella.

Grandpa tossed more potato into the frying pan and pointed it at Aiden. "I expect he's tired after falling in that bog."

Aiden nodded. The rest of them just ate.

"Anyway," said Grandma, hanging up her coat, "it's a beautiful day. Proper spring at last."

"Marvellous," said Grandpa, cracking two eggs into a bowl and gazing out of the window at the bright sunlit meadow stretching down to the sea. "What are those cows doing in the ploughed field?"

Grandma laughed. "Yes – bit of a rumpus going on about Mr Dempsey's cows. Apparently they opened a gate in the night and got into the bottom field."

Josh looked up at Chloe and watched her turn from white to red.

"How did that happen?" asked Aiden with an expression of innocence that Josh could only admire.

"I've no idea," said Grandma, smiling. "Oh, and I found this –" she held up Josh's red sweatshirt – "just in the entrance to Mr Dempsey's field. Is it yours, dear?" she asked, handing it to him.

This time Josh felt the blush race all the way up his back, over the top of his head and down to his chin.

On their own, after breakfast, Chloe sat on Ava's bed and watched in amazement as Ava took a sock from under the bed and shook out a cascade of diamonds. "Wow!" Chloe stood up, open-mouthed. "You found them!"

She ran her finger over the diamonds. In the morning sunshine they shone like gold. Their sharp sides reflected every scrap of the light in the room.

"And this one," said Ava, shaking the sock one more time.

A stone the size of a large hen's egg bounced on the coverlet. Flat on the front but cut many times on the sides, the stone was as clear as the sea around Gull Rock. Chloe bent over it, looking through it to see the bedspread pattern kaleidoscoped a million times. "I…" she began.

Ava smiled. "Yup."

"That's brilliant – does Aiden know?" asked Chloe.

Ava shook her head. Everyone had been fast asleep when she'd come back last night. It had been a slow journey home, creeping through hedges and farmyards, past sleeping dogs and cats. When she'd reached home Grandma and Grandpa had been snoozing in front of the telly and Ava had sneaked in past the open sitting-room door to slip up the staircase to bed.

She ran her fingers over the diamonds. She hadn't seen their real beauty until now. "I only found them when the man came up the stairs."

"What?" asked Chloe, lifting the largest diamond

and holding it up to the sunlight.

"When I heard him I had to go into the bathroom to hide. There wasn't anywhere except under the basin, so I squidged myself into this tiny space and held the bath mat in front of me."

Chloe raised one eyebrow. "They were hidden in the bath mat?"

"No!" Ava laughed. "They were hidden at the back underneath the basin. When I looked up there was this little bundle taped to the bottom of the pipe. I pulled it off and..." She pointed to the diamonds twinkling on the bed.

"Wow," said Chloe. "Wow."

CHAPTER 19

In the garden the sun shone and the little yellow celandine flowers glowed after yesterday's showers. Grandma's tulips were thinking about opening their blooms and thousands of green spikes were forcing their way through the red soil of the flower beds. It felt like a different season after yesterday's rain.

Chloe and Ava carried the diamonds out to the den and arranged them along the pallet. They looked incredible in the sunlight. Like stars.

"Wow!" said Aiden. "Just wow." He began to

count them. "And you're sure they didn't see you come back here?" he asked Ava.

She shook her head. "One hundred per cent sure. I was really careful. And guess what? I found the sheep."

"What? In the middle of the night?" asked her brother, picking up the Well of Beauty and holding it up to the light. The sunbeam broke into a thousand pieces and danced across the tree bark and the new green apple leaves.

"Where are they?" asked Aiden, climbing up on the pallet and looking down over the fields towards the clifftop cottages, where the men were stamping about, apparently searching the grass.

"In the conservatory at Sunny Grange House. I hid there."

Aiden nodded. "Clever place to hide them! So we can tell the police about that too."

"But we're still twelve diamonds short of a necklace," said Josh. The other three stared at him. "What? Well, we are, aren't we? I mean, we've sort of rescued it, but not completely."

"He's right," said Aiden. "We've half solved it. We could solve the whole thing. But at the moment we have no idea where we need to go."

The others looked at Chloe expectantly while she gazed anxiously into space. After a stupid number of minutes waiting for her to remember, Josh started picking splinters of wood from the crate, then Ava reached out and picked some blossom and mentioned Japan, and Chloe suddenly went red, then white, and started talking fast.

"Oh! I think maybe I've remembered it. When the woman was talking about the 'rest'. She said – oh, what did she say? She said something about the meeting. She said eleven… I was hiding under these daisies, and they were dripping down my back." Chloe stared towards the sea, trawling her memory.

Ava nodded. "And…"

"I had the path under my knees. She was on the phone to someone – probably Forty Grand." Chloe took the blossom from Ava and peeled the bud apart, laying the white petals against the bark of the apple tree. "Oh dear, I wish I could remember better, but it's definitely something Japanese."

"Did she mention a place?" Josh butted in. "Or are you trying to remember something you never heard?"

"Shh," said Ava. "Let her think."

Chloe puffed out her cheeks and blew the air out through her mouth.

Rather like a horse, Josh thought.

"I don't think she said exactly where, but she said something about a Japanese temple, or water garden, and –" Chloe reached forward as if she could grab the words – "an icehouse. She mentioned an icehouse."

"Morehamstone," said Aiden, turning back towards the house. "It's got to be Morehamstone. I'll just check."

Josh hung upside down from the apple tree, crossing his feet and staring at the sky through the network of blossom and buds. He couldn't believe Chloe had forgotten that. Personally, he thought, he would cycle up to Morehamstone and see if the woman turned up. Then he'd catch them all at once. But he was the youngest. What did he know?

Aiden returned with Bella at his side. He'd spoken to Grandpa, who'd confirmed that Morehamstone was the right house. He'd also made them a picnic that was now in Aiden's backpack.

Ava looked across the fields to see if the men were still there. Their car certainly was. That was when Chloe mentioned the second thing that Josh couldn't believe she'd forgotten.

"Oh! And look…" She held out a set of car keys.

"Who do they belong to?" asked Aiden.

Chloe pointed down towards the clifftop cottages, where the front door was open and the two men were still searching the garden.

They decided that Ava would ring the police. Then they'd get the police to arrest the men and then go over to Morehamstone and arrest the woman. Meanwhile Chloe and Aiden would get themselves there and delay the woman until the police arrived.

"What happens if the police don't believe us?" asked Josh.

"Or if we can't get them up there in time?" said Chloe.

Aiden glanced at Chloe. "I don't know." He swallowed. "But I'm sure we'll think of something."

CHAPTER 20

There was no rain and only the faintest breeze as Aiden and Chloe set off. Early butterflies played in the hedges. The verges bounced with greenery and the sun heated up the air. Chloe began to sweat soon after they started, but Aiden appeared heatproof. Lush green ferns lurked in the cool shadows every time they passed through any woodland and Chloe longed to stop and pour water over the back of her neck, but they kept going.

The garden didn't open until ten, so they had plenty of time and the ride was easier because they could hug the coast until they reached the garden. Morehamstone was a white house that faced out to sea in a creek filled with tree ferns and palms and secret dripping springs. There was an entrance down at the bottom by Moreham Beach but they pushed their bikes up the steep hill to the proper entrance and arrived at five to ten.

In the car park an elderly couple drank coffee from a thermos flask and a man in a green sweatshirt trimmed a hedge.

"Phew," said Chloe.

"Yup," said Aiden, peeling two iced buns from each other and stuffing most of one into his mouth while handing the other to Chloe.

They drank water, put their bikes in the bike rack, and waited for someone to start selling entry tickets from the booth.

Bees buzzed.

A distant cockerel crowed.

Chloe felt extremely anxious.

Somewhere nearby a bell struck ten and, as if summoned, a stream of cars flooded into the car park. Aiden swapped his bike helmet for a cap with a long peak and put on a pair of large sunglasses.

Chloe pulled on a flowery sunhat that she'd found in a drawer at the farm, which smelled only slightly of mothballs. Finishing the look, she balanced a pair of reflective green sunglasses on her nose. She looked, she thought, quite unlike herself, and hoped it would make her braver.

Glancing around, she couldn't see the red open-top car and wondered if she'd guessed right. They might not be meeting here at all. There were probably lots of places with Japanese gardens and icehouses. Although she couldn't think of any.

At the gate the woman gave them both tickets and a map. "And you can have a couple of these if you like," she said, beaming and handing them two rings made of bent willow.

"Er?" said Chloe, staring at the small circles and wondering quite what they were.

"You can make a crown! Pick greenery up and thread it through. Bring it back here for a photograph. We've had some very inventive entries."

"Oh," said Chloe, threading her arm through the rings and peering at a wall of photographs of children wearing lopsided leaf-hats.

"And don't forget the lambing in the top field. They're ever so sweet." The woman pinched her lips together as if to convey sweetness, but it looked as if she'd swallowed a lemon.

"Thank you," said Aiden, and they headed over the small lawn towards the entrance to the garden.

"Here," said Chloe. "Your crown."

"Thanks," said Aiden. "These'll give us a reason to crash about in the bushes."

"Hmm," said Chloe. "I suppose it's a sort of disguise." She scooped some ivy from a gardener's barrow and threaded it through the ring. It looked like a green jellyfish. A green forest jellyfish.

"C'mon, let's get down to the ponds and find a hiding place." Aiden stepped up the pace until they were almost running. They headed down the gravel path towards a series of streams that joined together to run down to the sea. A few families came in behind them and small children raced past them towards the tree ferns and the magical dells that surrounded them.

Checking that there was no sign of the woman or the two men, they stopped by the first of several ornamental ponds. Huge orange fish circled under cherry trees covered in blossom. From time to time the fish would break through the reflections of trees to gulp at insects on the surface.

It was all very still. Birds sang in the trees. The families had gone down towards the sea. It seemed like a setting waiting for something to happen.

"Here," said Chloe, skirting the water until she came to a huge clump of what looked like giant prickly rhubarb.

They crept into the gap between the vast leaves, finding themselves in a dry cavern of greenery. It felt like a secret place, somewhere that no one had ever found before.

CHAPTER 21

"Just do as I say," hissed Ava.

"Why should I?" said Josh.

"Oh my god. Because I say so, and because you're the youngest and I'm the oldest and…" She glared at him. "Because if you don't, I'll do something both of us might—"

Josh's lip jutted out. He was going to protest. Ava just knew it. "But they won't believe you. Grandma didn't believe me."

"All I want you to do is keep Grandma and Grandpa talking in the kitchen while I make a phone call." Ava seriously regretted keeping Josh with her. She should have thought of a reason for sending him with the others.

Josh, on the other hand, was ready to push Ava into a ditch and ride to find a police officer without her. "OK," said Josh. "I will, but you so owe me."

Ava shoved him into the kitchen, closed the door and, using all her acting skills, picked up the hall phone and rang the police.

The leaves were really quite prickly and the ground not as soft as it had at first appeared and Chloe was wondering just how they were going to keep the woman here if she came before the police arrived.

"We'll have to pretend to have lost something," said Aiden. "Or say you've got something in your eye. Or, I know, fall in the water. She'll have to pull you out."

"Hmm," said Chloe, looking at the pond, which appeared to be only knee-deep. "I've already done all that plaster stuff. She knows me."

"We'll think of something," said Aiden, adding more leaves to his crown.

Chloe parted the tall rhubarb leaves. "Oh no!"

she whispered. "Look."

Aiden peered over her shoulder. "Oh!"

It wasn't the woman; it was the men – and the two men had become three. Chloe knew it was them; Forty Grand was there, and Scottish Man, but now there was a third man and he didn't look very friendly. He was bigger and even uglier.

Chloe looked down at her phone. Ten twenty but no signal. She doubted very much that Ava and Josh had even managed to get hold of the police yet. And if they had, they'd probably still be explaining the whole thing. They almost certainly wouldn't know that the men weren't still at the cottage, so they'd go there to try to arrest them before coming up here.

She and Aiden would have to delay the gang, but there was every chance that the woman would turn up. She wished she'd called the police at the very beginning. This was turning from a crisis into a disaster.

She peered at the new man. He looked like a hired thug. He had arms that hung out from his sides, swinging, like a gorilla. His T-shirt was too small and his muscles too big. Chloe swallowed.

He could probably pick her up and throw her across the lake without even thinking. And they all looked really bad-tempered.

"Why are *they* here now?" said Aiden. "It's far too early."

"Maybe they're still hoping to get the money off her, even though they've lost the diamonds." Chloe pointed at the big man. "I wouldn't argue with him, would you?"

Aiden retreated into the prickly leaves. "We're going to have to think of something to delay them – and fast."

CHAPTER 22

In fact, it took nine minutes for the police car to arrive in the lane outside the farm and another ten to persuade the man and woman in charge of it that there wasn't time to tell their grandparents and, yes, they were deadly serious, and, yes, the dog was coming too. There'd been a bit of a gasp as Ava had revealed her sock full of treasure, and some doubt when they had explained about standing stones and long barrows.

Now they were in the police car and Josh felt mildly disappointed. It had been his lifetime's ambition to travel in a police car with the blue light flashing, but his dream was not to be realised because the policewoman wouldn't switch it on. Apparently it wasn't necessary. She still drove pretty fast, though, and he had to clutch Bella tight to stop her flying across the back seat.

They stopped at the clifftop cottages and the policeman rushed round to the back of the house while the policewoman went to the front door. "Stay here, you two," she said.

Josh looked once again at the car parked out the front. He thought of the keys hanging from a twig in their tree house and smiled.

"No one in," said the policeman, coming back. "Door was open, so I had a nosy about and I couldn't find anything to even suggest there was anyone staying here." He came over and, putting one hand on the roof of the car, leaned in. "Are you sure about this, kids? Are you sure those diamonds are real? Serious offence, you know, wasting police time."

"We're a hundred per cent sure," said Ava, speaking too fast. "I'm really sorry, but if you think there's no one there, that means we need to get up to Morehamstone, and, like, really quickly."

"Excuse me," said Chloe, her heart in her mouth. "I've got a message for you."

Two of the men turned to face her. Forty Grand seemed to ignore her completely.

"Not now, little girl," said the third man. Chloe began to take mental notes immediately. *Not very nice. London accent. Unshaven*. She sniffed. *Maybe even unwashed*.

"But I think it's important; the lady gave me ten pounds," said Chloe, trying really hard not to blush. She hated lying, her blushes always gave her away, but she hoped the men might just think she was overheating.

"What lady?" said Scottish Man, suddenly paying her more attention.

"Yeah, what lady?" asked Forty Grand.

"Well," said Chloe, putting her back to the lake so that the men turned to her and wouldn't see Aiden creep out of the huge rhubarb and off up the hill towards a small thatched building. "She was wearing these red high heels, and a black mac…" There was no reaction from the men and she realised they'd probably never seen the woman. "And she said something about meeting to hand stuff over, that you'd be here by the lake, but she'd rather do whatever it is somewhere less public." Chloe closed her mouth and hoped very much that she hadn't said too much. Or too little.

This time the policewoman put on the blue light and drove fast – so fast that Josh actually thought his scrambled eggs might come back up all over the scat in front of him. Even the policeman in the passenger seat gripped the dashboard so hard that his fingers turned white.

"Whoa!" said Ava, an excited grin crossing her face. She loved going fast; it didn't matter whether it was in a car or on a bike. Josh had never seen her so excited.

While the siren blared, they shot up the hill past the farm, and out on to the top road. The policeman fiddled with a bank of electronic stuff that Josh imagined was the police radio. He pressed lots of buttons and held a little speaker to his mouth.

"Are there other police if they're needed?" asked Josh.

"They're all looking for the sheep," said the policeman.

"Sheep?" said Ava. "I know where they are – in the Sunny Grange House conservatory – or at least they were last night."

"Seriously?" said the policeman, pointing back over his shoulder. "Where we've just been?" He fiddled with the radio and started to speak to someone on the other end about the sheep.

"And what do these jewel thieves look like?" asked the policewoman, taking a corner at speed.

"Oh, ugly," said Josh.

"I don't really know," said Ava. "Never actually seen them properly."

"Ugly," repeated the policeman, copying the information into his pocket book.

"One of them wears a yellow top." Josh checked his notebook. "One of them's Scottish. They went to those cottages we've just visited, and then Ava…" Josh stopped and looked at his sister.

She glared back.

"Ava what?" asked the policeman.

"I got the diamonds, these ones…" She waved the sock at the policeman. "I got them back from the men."

"How?" he asked as they swung round, first right, then left.

Luckily it was at that point that a herd of cows began to cross the road and the policewoman had to slam on the brakes, sending the diamonds spinning out of the sock and arcing through the car. They bounced off the roof, catching the sunlight, falling like magical raindrops all around Josh and Ava's heads. The Well of Beauty landed neatly in the cold dregs of a cup of coffee jammed in the cup holder and the others scattered across the upholstery and the floor.

"Oh!" said the policeman, fishing about in the coffee, retrieving the diamond and rubbing it on an old tissue. "Where were we? Oh yes, so you got the diamonds."

"Some of the diamonds, these diamonds – not the first few diamonds," explained Ava, scrabbling around on the floor and whisking them away from Bella's interested tongue. "The first twelve diamonds went to the woman in the red car with the high heels." She leaned forward to pick up a diamond that had wedged itself in the air vent.

"And she came from the pub," said Josh. "The Three Witches on the moor."

"But, hang on," said the policewoman, "that's not where we're going? Is it?"

"No – we're going to Morehamstone because that's where they're meeting. Only the men didn't have a car, so they must have taken a taxi or something to get there."

"Or they've got friends," said the policeman.

"Or they've got friends," repeated Josh, realising that even though they now had two police officers, Chloe and Aiden might be in real danger.

CHAPTER 23

"So the thing is," said Chloe, wandering slowly up the path towards the little wooden house at the top, "it's all because my cousin's allergic to fish…"

"What?" said Scottish Man, who was struggling with the slight slope. "All fish?"

"Fish with bones," said Chloe, wondering what on earth she was saying.

"She's allergic to fish with bones?" said Forty Grand, stopping to stare. "What?"

"Oh," said Chloe, desperately trying to think of anything to say. "I don't mean fish, I mean crustaceans. You know, shellfish." She was wittering on; she knew it. But she needed to behave like a girl who had no cares and no idea that she was leading a gang into a trap. She needed to walk fast enough to make sure that they didn't meet the woman in the red car if she should arrive, but slowly enough to make sure that Aiden could be ready to spring the trap. If he could spring the trap.

They'd had no time to make a proper plan, so this was the best they could do. But the little house was perfect. Rumour had it that some mad baron had kept a bear in it a couple of hundred years ago. She glanced back at the big man. He was certainly a bear. She just hoped that the little house really did have bars over the windows like she'd imagined.

"So the thing is," she heard herself saying for the thousandth time, "it means we eat a lot of cheese sandwiches."

"What you on about?" said Forty Grand, who seemed to have developed a facial tic since meeting Chloe.

She took them the long way, pointing out various landmarks, dogs' graves, ponds of toads, and tree ferns, and finally led them round a group of pine trees into a woodland glade. Wild garlic stretched under the trees, filling the air with a pungent perfume, and Chloe thought how much she wished she was sitting on the little bench under the huge pine trees, gazing at the view and smelling the flowers. Instead she glanced up at Forty Grand. He looked as if he was going to explode.

"Anyway," she said, trying to sound normal, "you can see the hut." She pointed up the path to the little thatched building. "I hope you have a nice meeting with the lady. I'm going to find my mum. Bye!" She waved and ran off to the right, away from the little house.

"Hey!" Forty Grand called, but Chloe just flapped a hand in a kind of half wave and picked up speed, so that by the time she reached the stone gateway at the other end of the path she was sprinting. She ducked through the arch and turned up the hill, running half crouched behind the low wall so that they wouldn't be able to see her. To her right bluebells stretched away into the woods, creating a blue haze where there were distant families exclaiming at the carpet of flowers, none of them near enough to be of any help. Then at the end of the wall she swung round on to another path hidden between borders of spiky leaves that would lead her to the back of the hut and Aiden.

Only just missing an ancient lady and her equally ancient husband, the police car skidded to a halt in the car park at Morehamstone, pinging gravel against all the cars.

"Red Shoes?" asked Ava.

"No," said Josh, hanging half out of his window. "Don't think she's here yet."

"Should we hide the police car?" asked Ava.

The policeman frowned. "Why?" he said, stuffing the sock and the diamonds that they had managed to retrieve into the glove compartment.

"Because if the woman comes, she'll take one look at it and disappear. She's got the rest of the necklace—"

"And the rest of the money," said Josh.

The policeman stared at them as if trying to work out if they were spinning some elaborate story or telling the truth. "OK. I'll take you round to the farm shop. You can wait here in the car until we come back."

"I'll see you in the garden in ten." The policewoman grabbed her hat and headed towards the entrance, talking into her radio.

"But you can't leave us here; you won't know who you're looking for," complained Josh as the policeman started the engine.

The policeman looked at them in the mirror. He didn't say anything, just turned the car and drove it to the farm shop entrance, parking it at the far end of the car park out of sight.

"You have a point," he said.

"I do?" said Josh, beaming.

"Come on then, but behave," he said, opening the door.

Aiden was behind the hut. He heard Chloe's feet thundering on the path behind him and he waved to slow her down. It was too loud. The men might hear her.

Distant laughter came from the families enjoying the bluebell woods, but it was drowned out by the heavy footsteps on the gravel path in front of the hut. Then there were voices – male voices. They were chatting to each other in low tones and he got the feeling that Forty Grand was in a really foul mood.

He'd checked the hut. The windows were metal, but not really barred. He figured it might hold them for a few minutes.

Once again he glanced at his phone. Eight minutes to eleven.

Chloe crawled down next to him. She'd overheated and was flapping her hands to cool herself down.

Aiden put his finger to his lips and Chloe nodded.

They listened for the sound of feet on the floorboards.

One set.

Two sets.

Where was the third man?

The voices rumbled from inside and then they could hear hands brushing the walls and roof, searching. Then came another set of feet thumping up the path.

"Ready?" whispered Aiden.

"Yup," breathed Chloe, and they ran to the front of the hut, leaned on the door, closed it, bolted it and ran as fast as they could down the hill.

CHAPTER 24

It felt important to be waved through the entrance gate and Ava might have enjoyed it, but she was starting to worry about Chloe and Aiden. They'd taken ages to get up here, and it might be that the woman in the red car had been and gone. But Chloe had been sure about eleven, and it was only ten to.

The policewoman was talking to one of the gardeners, who pointed off down the main path, and the four of them moved through the garden, checking and listening and generally frightening small children and families.

"The actual pond thing's down there," said Josh. "Where we think they're supposed to be meeting." He took Bella to look inside an enormous rhubarb plant, and Ava and the policewoman checked a clump of bamboo.

They moved through the garden searching everywhere as they went, and Ava began to wonder if Aiden and Chloe were actually here. They might not have made it to Morehamstone at all. They might have taken another route and be stuck somewhere on the way. She was still worrying when she made it to the ornamental ponds and spotted Chloe and Aiden arriving on the other side.

"Quick!" called Aiden over the water. "We've got the men in the bear house. It won't hold them for long."

"Show us," said the policeman, following him up the track while the policewoman started talking into her radio.

A second later there was a terrible sound of smashing glass. Everyone in the garden froze and looked up towards the little hut.

"C'mon!" yelled Aiden, racing up the path,

closely followed by Chloe, Josh, Bella and the policewoman.

The policeman had opened the door, and was trying to get a handcuff on Forty Grand, but the Scottish Man was clambering out of the window and a huge man Ava had never seen before had armed himself with a bench.

"Josh! Chloe!" she yelled, pointing to Scottish Man, who was already heading off in the direction of the icehouse.

"Yes!" yelled Chloe, running after him, with Josh alongside her.

Forty Grand punched the policeman in the jaw and charged out of the bear house straight past Aiden.

Ava raced up the slope.

"Mine!" shouted Aiden ahead of her and they both swung to follow him.

They ran pace for pace through the woods and out on to the main lawn, right through a guided tour, swerving round some people in a golf buggy, and then back into the orchard, getting closer and closer with every step. Suddenly Bella leaped alongside them, her lead trailing, her legs faster than anyone else's.

"Hey!" shouted someone who looked vaguely official, but Ava ignored him, digging for an extra turn of speed that she didn't know she had.

Forty Grand swung up out of the orchard into a small garden laid out with neat beds. He charged up the middle, Aiden following, and Ava took one of the side paths, getting ahead of him and turning to face him at the end.

He stopped, leaning forward, sucking in air. "Kids, get out of the way; you don't know what you're dealing with."

"You're not passing me," said Ava, dodging from side to side and flicking a glance at Aiden behind the man.

"Oh, come on," said the man. "Stop playing silly beggars."

The man sidestepped, which was when Bella lunged, grabbing the man's ankle in her jaws and bringing him down heavily into the only prickly rose bush in the border.

Beyond the icehouse was a path that lead to the sea. It headed straight down through sheer woodland and Scottish Man almost managed to lose Chloe and Josh, but they knew the path better, cutting off corners and catching up with him at the bottom. He rushed out into the tiny harbour, startling a woman and tangling himself in a pushchair before crashing into a pile of lobster pots.

Chloe took her chance. She grabbed a fishing net and threw it over the man. Josh took the other side and the lady with the pushchair hit him over the head with a plastic spade. Then they sat on him and waited for a passing family to help them get him back up the hill to the police car.

With the help of two gardeners, and Bella's teeth, Aiden tied Forty Grand's hands together with his belt and between them all they led him back towards the main entrance. Their captive swore and kicked the whole way. When they reached the front, another police car had arrived, and Scottish Man was sitting looking desperate in the back.

"Snotty kids," said Forty Grand, kicking at a stone mushroom and wincing.

Near the entrance to the garden a policewoman ran towards them. "Another one, eh?" she said, snapping a handcuff over one of his wrists and attaching the other end to a railing. "Well done, kids, you're doing better than we are – look!"

Aiden followed the direction of her pointing finger to the thatched hut. Three police officers were still trying to get the third man out. But with occasional roars and more smashing glass, wood and possibly police, it sounded like he was successfully fighting them off.

"Will there be any more police cars?" Ava asked.

The policewoman shook her head. "I'm afraid that's all there are of us. I don't expect any more will come. Still, they'll have him in custody soon, and then we can all go home."

"It's just…" began Ava.

"There!" yelled Josh, pointing down the hill past the house to the lane.

"Oh my god!" said Ava, brushing past the policewoman and tearing towards the visitor centre.

"Oh no!" said Aiden, and handed Bella's lead to the policewoman.

"What?" said the policewoman, but she was too

slow. All four of the cousins had begun to run, their feet pounding the grass, racing each other towards the red car that had just pulled in to the car park.

CHAPTER 25

There was no plan, but Aiden knew that they had to keep the woman there. He also knew that the moment she saw the policewoman with the handcuffed members of the gang she'd run and probably disappear forever. But how were they going to stop her?

The woman clambered out of her car and looked around. She wore dark glasses and a hat, but this time she was wearing flat shoes and jeans and looked much more ordinary. In fact, if it hadn't been for the car, Aiden wouldn't have known who she was. Reaching into the back seat for a large black holdall, she checked her phone. It obviously didn't tell her anything she didn't already know and she wandered towards the main entrance.

As she turned her back on the car, Josh emerged from behind the bins, swooped past the little plant sale area, grabbed a tall metal stake with a wonky robin on the end of it and threaded it through the holes in the two front wheels, connecting one side to the other and effectively disabling it.

Genius, thought Aiden. When the woman tried to set off, the metal rod would tangle one side with the other. It probably wouldn't do too much damage, but it would almost certainly stop her going anywhere. It was almost perfect. It was a shame about the metal robin apparently glued to the outside of the tyre, but Chloe, shooting out from behind Josh, had thought of that. She swooped over with an armful of grass cuttings that she artfully scattered around the tyre as a disguise. Both cousins melted back into their hiding places.

The woman was searching her handbag while strolling across the gravel drive and hadn't noticed any of this. With barely a break in her stride she wandered to the visitor centre and went inside.

"Quick!" hissed Ava. "Chloe, Josh – the police."

Aiden watched his cousins slide through a narrow gap in the hedge and run round the side of the house. He and Ava stood up and followed the woman. If they kept her within arm's reach, then hopefully they could stop her running away.

The lone policewoman had somehow acquired a cup of tea and was chatting to a gardener. Chloe thought she looked far too relaxed for a woman guarding two jewel thieves.

"We need you to arrest someone," said Josh.

"What? Another one?" she said. And then she said to the gardener. "These kids are amazing."

"Aren't they just?" said the gardener, ruffling Josh's hair.

Josh shook off the hand. He hated people ruffling his hair.

"We need you now," said Chloe, pointing the policewoman in the right direction.

"And why am I arresting her?" asked the policewoman.

"For wearing stupid shoes?" suggested Josh.

"Handling stolen goods," said Chloe, pressing gently on her cousin's foot.

The policewoman marched into the visitor centre, and Chloe and Josh linked arms behind her, blocking the entrance into the garden. Opposite them Ava and Aiden did the same, closing off the other exit.

The woman turned from one side to the other looking for an escape. "What's going on?" she said, and then she spotted Chloe. "You!" she said. "You brat!" And she raised her handbag to swipe at her, but the policewoman grabbed her arm and clicked on the handcuffs. "Now, now – hitting a child, madam? Enough of that! I'm arresting you…"

CHAPTER 26

The man behind the counter in the visitor centre looked bewildered. "Jewel thieves," said Josh casually, as if it happened every day, and the man nodded as if he understood.

The woman with the red car was led away to the police car, and Ava watched her go. She wanted to know if they were going to find the rest of the diamonds. She wanted to know where the woman came from and who the diamonds had been stolen for. But she knew that was something she might actually have to leave to the police.

The original policeman came down, dishevelled and sweating. "Was that man difficult to catch?" asked Josh.

The policeman nodded. "Yes, very. But I think my colleagues have it under control – I just thought I'd buy you kids an ice cream each. To say thank you for all your hard work."

The man behind the counter opened the top of the freezer cabinet and the cousins reached in. Josh took a giant choc ice that Ava knew would melt before he got to the end, Chloe read each wrapper to make sure it was vegetarian, and Aiden chose something sensible and cheap.

Ava chose an ice lolly. She was thirsty, and she was just eyeing up the bottles of cold drinks when she heard a shout from the garden. Looking up, she saw some sandwiches flying through the air as a woman staggered backwards towards the ornamental ponds, and she saw Bella break free from her lead and the huge bear man charging straight for them.

The policeman stepped forward to block his path, but he was thrown aside by the man, who picked up speed and belted through to the visitor centre like an out-of-control bowling ball.

The cousins handed their ice creams to the man behind the counter and lined the route.

"Now!" yelled Aiden. Ava launched herself and clutched the man's leg just behind the knee, while Aiden did the same on the other side. Simultaneously Josh and Chloe leaped up to grab his arms, so that by the time he cannoned into the leaflet carousel he was almost horizontal.

Bella leaped in for the kill, closing her jaws round the man's ear.

"Wowee!" said Josh, appearing from under a mountain of leaflets. "That was close."

More police officers arrived. Some of them asked questions. Some of them poked around in the red car. The day grew hot.

Two policemen in white suits crawled around in the bottom of the police car, searching for the diamonds that had flown out of the sock during the journey. Chloe watched them, thinking about her bike, and the ride home, and whether they would finish any time soon because it was turning into a lovely afternoon and they could go down to the beach at Moreham and paddle.

"Can we go home yet?" she asked.

"Not yet, I'm afraid," said one of the policemen.

"Check under the mats, and down the crack at the back of the seat," said Josh, leaning in through the door of the police car.

They ignored him, and soon another man in a white all-over-suit-thing began to photograph and arrange the diamonds in a long string on a stone wall. He peered at them very carefully, counting and recounting.

He looked over to the children, a frown on his face.

"What's the matter?" asked Ava.

"Well, there's one missing – has anyone taken it? A souvenir perhaps?"

"No," said Ava. "Just – no."

Josh's eyes widened. "We'd never do something like that – it must be in the car somewhere."

It was when he leaned forward to peer inside the car that Chloe spotted a small glinting thing by his collar.

"Oh!" she exclaimed, picking out what seemed to be a piece of glass.

Josh stood open-mouthed. "What?" he said. "How?"

"Ah, thank you," said the policeman, smiling. "Thank you very much. Now you can all go home."

CHAPTER 27

A police Land Rover gave them a lift back to the farm. Chloe stuck her arms out of the window, feeling the cool wind and the hot sun run through the gaps between her fingers. The countryside bounced past. Small lambs clustered around their mothers, and calves ran kicking and skipping over the fields. Fledglings dive-bombed the road behind. The countryside was beautiful and growing more amazing with every sunlit hour. Chloe felt huge untempered happiness at being here, at being part of it.

They came up to the moor and went down the other side, and through the windscreen Drake's Bay opened up in front of them, sunlight on the water, with Thorn Island sitting like a green jewel in a silver setting. A lone fishing trawler headed out from the harbour and disappeared into the bright shimmer of the horizon.

The policewoman driving them pulled in to the farm track. "Well, if you're sure you don't want me to come in," she said, stopping at the entrance. "I could tell your grandparents how totally brilliant you've been."

"Honestly," said Aiden, "we don't want to worry them. Thanks for the ice creams."

"And the lift," said Chloe, handing down her bike and then Aiden's. "I've had enough cycling for one day."

"Thank you all. Take care," said the policewoman, swinging the Land Rover round and waving as she headed off up the hill.

Aiden shoved the bikes back into the bike shed, and all four cousins wandered up to the farm, instantly hooked by the smell of baking that was floating out of the back door.

"Delicious," said Ava.

"Yum," said Chloe.

"Mine," said Josh, breaking into a trot that became a canter and finally a full-on gallop.

"Goodness," said Grandma, holding the back door open as they streamed past. "How do you children always know when the scones are out of the oven?"

For a moment they all sat quietly, concentrating on spreading rich cream across the hot scones.

"Cream then jam," said Josh, slapping the thick white cream over the scone and then dropping a dab of raspberry jam in the middle.

"Nah – jam then cream," said Aiden, melting the jam into the scone and arranging a delicate circle of cream on top.

"Either way," said Ava, taking a huge bite and smearing cream across her chin while the others laughed.

Chloe thought how different eating scones round the table was from chasing jewel thieves across the countryside. She spread jam on the cream and nibbled the edge, savouring the flavour.

The cousins sank back into their chairs and

chewed, and rubbed their scuffed knees and elbows and said nothing.

"Oh, I've just remembered," said Grandma, sitting down at the table. "We had a phone call from the police. Guess what?"

Panicked, Aiden looked across at Ava. "I can't. What is it?"

"Apparently, Ava dear, it was you that found the sheep! And Arrowhead Moor House would like to reward you for finding them, so they've offered you all free tickets to the Arrowhead Moor House Adventure. Isn't that marvellous?" She looked round the table. None of the cousins looked very excited.

"Goodness, you're all very cool about it," said Grandpa. "When I was your age I'd have been thrilled to win an adventure. Apparently you get to follow loads of clues and go on a zip wire."

"It's just—" started Josh.

Ava kicked him under the table. "It's just that we've had a very exciting time already this holiday."

"Have you?" said Grandpa. "What's happened so far then?"

"Um…" Ava looked round the table.

"We caught the jewel thieves," said Josh. "It was *reeeally* dangerous."

"Did you?" said Grandma, laughing and not believing a word. "That's terrific. I love your stories, Josh." She ruffled his hair.

Josh glared.

"Where did you find the sheep?" Grandpa wiped a blob of cream from his plate and popped it in his mouth.

"They were in the conservatory at Sunny Grange House."

"How marvellous! But how did you find them there?" asked Grandpa. "I thought that place was closed for the spring?"

Ava stared desperately at Chloe.

"We were walking past?" said Chloe, glancing desperately at Aiden.

"What's the weather going to be like tomorrow?" said Aiden, jumping up from the table and switching on the radio.

"And, in further news, after a dramatic series of arrests in an ornamental garden, the gang that stole the Eliza Necklace have been captured and the necklace recovered. Malcolm Angus reports from the scene…"

Aiden turned down the volume. "Actually, Grandma, that Arrowhead Moor House Adventure thing sounds really exciting," he said. "How do we get it? Do we all have to go up there? We could set off now if you like."

Hours later, after Grandpa had driven Ava and Chloe to Arrowhead Moor House and they'd come back with the tickets for the adventure, and when they'd eaten some chocolate and Josh had eaten all the chocolate that he could possibly stuff in his mouth, they lay in their tree house staring up at the blue tarpaulins and listening to a little fresh spring rain pattering on the plastic.

"That was an awesome twenty-four hours," said Aiden. "Scary and excellent."

"I can't believe that Little Miss Perfect broke into a house," said Josh.

"If you mean me, I don't believe it either," said Ava, flapping her face with her hand.

"And weren't those diamonds amazing?" said Chloe. "I mean, they belonged to Queen Victoria. Queen Victoria might actually have worn them."

"S'pose so," said Josh, unimpressed.

They gazed out at the rain.

"It was …" started Ava, "… sooooo exciting. Racing through the lanes with the siren and the car all over the place was…" She shivered at the memory.

Josh rolled on to his back. He said something that the others couldn't quite hear.

"What?" asked Ava.

"Isn't that why we're here?" He rolled back over, crossed his legs and sat up. "This farm, this bay. This countryside where all the adventures happen." He stood up and filled the entrance of their shelter, stretching his arms wide so that they reached both sides. He laughed and then shouted, "We're probably in the very best place in the whole world!"

More fantastic fiction from Nosy Crow!

A funny, heart-warming adventure filled with goats, secrets, bat poo, a big storm, family and laughter.

Funny fiction from Nosy Crow!

A hilarious and spooky series
packed with ghosts, gadgets
and outrageous battles!